ALIEN'S CAPTIVE

Earth Brides & Alien Warriors

TINA MOSS

ALIEN'S CAPTIVE
Earth Brides & Alien Warriors, Book 1

TINA MOSS
www.tinamoss.com

Cover Design by MilbArt. All stock photos licensed appropriately.

Edited by Danielle DeVor & Yelena Casale.

For information on subsidiary rights, please contact the publisher at info@tinamoss.com.

2nd Edition. Originally published by City Owl Press.

Print Edition ISBN: 978-1-964370-01-9

Digital Edition ISBN: 978-1-964370-00-2

Printed in the United States of America

PRAISE FOR TINA MOSS

"The sexual tension between two supernatural special agents, one a feisty shape-shifter, the other an aristocratic vampire, spices up the excellent second *Paranormal Crimes Division* romance, *Red Alert*. A combination of flirtatious banter, sizzling chemistry, and edge-of-your-seat storytelling make this a sure bet."
— *Publishers Weekly Starred Review*

"*A Touch of Darkness* rockets you along a pulse-pounding story and sucks you into the characters. You'll want to cheer for Cassie's feisty spirit and loyalty, and you'll come to love Gabe and all his wonderful flaws."
— *Award Winning Fantasy Author, Heather McCorkle*

"A thrilling and well-crafted debut novel…a full throttle ride, complete with several twists and turns."
— *The Book Chick*

"This new paranormal urban fantasy series is a mesmerizing and intriguing read. *The Key Series* is a fascinating world of angels, fallen angels and demons with some unique elements and surprising twists."
— *Evampire*

"An imaginative twist on the concept of angels and demons, complete with the requisite conflicts between duty and love, as well as the issues of loyalty and betrayal."
— *Night Owl Reviews*

To all those who look at the night sky and dream of the worlds beyond. May the stars align for you.

Author's Note

I cannot thank you enough for picking up this book. I want you to feel safe and secure when reading. As such, I've included a list of content information available on my website at: www.tinamoss.com/content-info/

If you have any concerns about the contents of this book, please be sure to check that page first. Thank you again and happy reading!

Chapter 1

AVA

I WAS INSIDE STELLA'S DOG CRATE. AND MY HEAD pounded like the morning after a night spent drowning in my research—and too much red wine. Why those thoughts came to mind as I blinked my eyelids open? No idea. Slowly, I pushed aside the remnants of my messy bun to find a lump. Apple-shaped and tender to the touch, it had to be the source of my headache.

Genius deduction, professor. What other gems did you glean from that? I shook my head at the question, sending a fresh rush of pain to my temple and neck.

I hissed through my teeth. The pain was awful, but it distracted me. *Classic coping mechanism,* I thought bitterly. My head throbbed harder. Yeah, that psych degree was paying off now. Nothing like self-diagnosis in the midst of a crisis. I sucked in a breath. *In, two, three. Out, two, three.*

"Okay, then, stop stalling and assess," I said it aloud to ground myself. I'd already registered the cage. Thin metal wires twisted around each other like the threads of a fine woven rug. Except these strands created braided bars that ran vertical and parallel to each other. My face rested on the bottom panel where I laid in a tight ball. Metal beneath my cheek, metal braids around me. I sat up, jostling the delicate balance between numbness and blinding pain. It zapped behind my eyes this time.

"Damn it." I chanced looking up. The crown of my head to the cage's top panel was less than an arm's length away. I reached for it, needing to know if it too was as infallible as it looked. My fingers grazed more metal.

Reality crept in, its edges toying with my senses.

I wasn't in my sweet Samoyed's crate. I couldn't be. Stella was with my parents back on Earth. The big fluffy mush had wanted to come with me on the trip. I had seen it in my girl's sad eyes when we had to say goodbye. But space was no place for a dog. I wasn't even sure if it was a place for humans. But I wanted to find out. That was my goal in taking the job. After endless hours of researching the human condition, I needed to escape theory for practice.

Yeah, you escaped all right. Look where you are now? I bit my tongue. I could have taken that teaching position on the Big Island, one of Earth's last paradise refuges after the atmospheric holes made most of the planet inhabitable.

But no. I didn't want to go back into the classroom. It was the mysteries of space for me. And now, where was I?

I stared through the metal bars. "Yeah, where am I?"

Darkness pervaded the space. I could make out a thin strip of light from under a doorway. But even that seemed strange, as if the door were curved somehow. The air smelled stagnant like it had been trapped too long in one place. Well, I could relate.

So badly I had wanted to escape my humdrum life, to have a shot at a real adventure and maybe, even make a difference in the world. When the Unicus power couple offered me a seat on the first deep space flight, I didn't hesitate for a second. Their company helped humanity's survival, and they wanted me—*me*—to aid in the creation of an off-world colony. It was everything I'd dreamed. My civilization psychology expertise, sociology degree, hell even the old undergrad anthropology classes would come in handy. It was like I'd built my entire professional life for that chance.

And now, it was gone.

Tears stung the backs of my eyes, but I placed my palms firmly over my lids and refused to let them fall. *You're not done yet. Think!*

I took another shuddering breath and tried to sort through my thoughts. The last thing I remembered was having coffee in the ship's mess hall. We'd been about four months out at that point and past the solar system. The stars had appeared even brighter so far from home, and yet, they felt incredibly lonely. Like me. It had always been difficult for me to connect with others, preferring books to friends. But this trip had been an opportunity to connect with like-minded people. The crew were efficient, and my fellow scientists, experts, and such were nice enough. Still, I'd been…disconnected. It was like being an extra in a movie. Even when I had a speaking line, it rang hollow.

As I'd sat alone, sipping the caffeine elixir that forced a small smile from my otherwise glum mood, an alarm blasted through the ship. "All hands to stations. All hands to stations." The mug had fallen from my grip, cracking on the table and spilling coffee all over the floor. I'd hopped back in time to avoid the mess on my jumper. Not that the solid gray one-piece wouldn't be improved by some color. Still, I'd managed to get my feet under me and run toward… Where was I supposed to go?

Before I could figure it out, something hard and heavy slammed into the ship.

The impact sent me careening through the mess hall as the ship dove at a harsh angle. My shoulder collided with the bottom of the table, a ringing noise sounded in my ears, and then nothing.

Pulling at the front zipper on my jumper in the present, I angled the garment down my left shoulder. Mottled purple bruises ran almost to my elbow. I sighed and readjusted my clothes. No matter how hard I tried, I could recall nothing more.

We must have been attacked. It was the only way to explain my current confinement.

As I came to terms with that realization, a burst of light from the curved doorway illuminated the space. I blinked against it, waiting for my eyes to adjust.

When they did, I wished they hadn't.

A creature stood before me unlike any I'd ever seen. It had to be almost seven feet tall with a round body encased in an insect-like shell, long spindly legs, and four lanky arms topped with lobster-style claws. My gaze traveled up to a face with a pair of antennas, wicked mandibles, and egg-sized eyes.

I screamed.

"Ceassse your whining, ssslave," the bug-man hissed at me.

It took my mouth a half second to catch up with my brain, and I continued to scream, until… "I understand you?" Humanity had long been capable of translation technology. Babbler units were the most popular, often installed in the brain stem at birth with an adjuster function behind the right ear lobe. I knew all this, and yet, the sheer shock of comprehending this bug-man's words tossed me to the stone age.

"It isss clear you do." The insect-monster stalked closer and opened my cage door.

Oh hell no. I shrunk to the back of the metal contraption, as far as I could get from the bug beast. I knew the possibility of aliens when I started the journey into space. What none of my fellow space travelers or I counted on were bugs-based aliens. I didn't even like bumblebees, and at least they were important for the ecosystem.

Okay, I was spiraling. This was a panic attack waiting to happen.

Breathe.

When that lobster-like claw reached inside the cage, no amount of self-talk would keep the fear at bay. I screamed and did not stop. That didn't prevent the creature from latching onto my ankle and pulling me through the opening. I grabbed at the braided bars, not caring for a second how they cut into my palms.

"Let go!" I held on with everything I had.

It didn't help.

"Foolisssh Terran." Bug-man tugged me free like I weighed nothing. He dragged me toward the curved doorway and beyond, only releasing his grip after I'd been thoroughly caked in dirt. "Now, you will behave."

I scrambled to my knees. Everything throbbed. My head had never stopped, and now, I could add an overall ache to the growing list of injuries. Trying to ignore my pain, I looked around to get a better idea of my circumstances. A translucent wall surrounded me in a full circle like a fishbowl of thick plastic. The ground was all dirt, and to the side the bug-man stood, calling in his loud hissing voice, "Ssspecial treatsss today!"

My brows rose toward my hairline.

He glanced at me, the bulbous eyes growing larger, and a sick smirk twisting his thin lips. "Fresssh and rare!"

Nausea threatened to bring up the coffee I'd had who knew how long ago. Tears threatened, starting at the corners, but I wouldn't let them fall. Not yet. I had to think of how the hell to get out of this mess.

From beyond the translucent wall, another figure stood. Almost the size of the bug-man, I could make out his dark brown hair. He appeared to be more humanoid, but it was hard to tell as the fishbowl effect of the wall distorted everything on the outside. Either that or this new figure was built like a pretzel.

If that was the case, I'd still take my chances with twisty humanoid over bug-man. I started to crawl toward the newcomer when the bug-man skulked toward me, his lobster fist raised. "You think to essscape?"

This time there was no stopping the tears or the cry that tore from my heart.

I was never going home.

Chapter 2

XELAN

I cursed the carriage's creaking wheel. It slowed our progress and grated my ears. With the latest rescues tucked inside the ancient conveyance, we could afford no delay. One of the former slaves was heavy with child, and she needed the safety of our ship to deliver. With spies everywhere on Craxon, unloading our quarry had become increasingly difficult. Even the weather was against us as the air had grown frosty, turning the typical warmth of the planet to a biting chill. We had to make the meeting spot soon and get our charges off this Celestia forsaken planet.

"Crex," I muttered and yanked on the reins of my catar —a six-legged beast of burden. Waving to my fellow warrior, I signaled for Brokdar to take the lead ahead of me. "Continue on."

Brok's gaze cut to me. The large Rhonar warrior was the stoic type. Speaking more in action than words, he kept his catar at the front, but inclined his head to the side and grumbled, "Trouble, Xelan?"

"Checking on the drav wheel." I backed my beast to the side of the carriage and motioned to our trusted Kinsian attendants, Maena and Tallis, to keep the vehicle moving. "Stay on guard."

The couple nodded, driving the antiquated contraption as it sputtered along.

The wheel threatened to fall from its spoke at any hard bump in the road. Eying it sharply, I reckoned a quick shot from my blaster would hold the thing until I could fix it. I took aim and hit dead center. Yet, the small victory gave me little relief from the emptiness gnawing inside me, a curse of my kind. I had no time to dwell, however, on the state of my existence. For a slimy muck permeated my mind, filling it with an emotion I recognized as greed.

The taste of it slid over my tongue, causing me to gag in response. *Disgusting.* I shook my head to dislodge the feelings. While Rhonar warriors all suffered the same fate of our biology—two stages that caused an all consuming hunger, followed by a sucking void—I had an added curse. Each warrior possessed a unique ability, but I never considered mine a great gift. No, I was destined to experience the emotions of others. Useful in a fight to judge my opponents, true, but a hellish nightmare when I couldn't block it out.

With the slave pens coming into view and the prior frustration from the issues with the wheel, I hadn't raised my empathic shields in time. The suffering of the slaves, the greed of the slavers, and the desire of the customers combined in a sickening emotional soup.

"Sale! Sale! Priced just right," a shout rang from the outer edge of the slavers' pens. "Get all your needs met with our prime selection."

The Palaxian stew I had for breakfast churned in my gut. Brok and I had spent many cycles undercover, experiencing all three of this planet's seasons: hot and dry, warm and wet, and now, the frost. I posed as a wealthy merchant of the Elite class, and Brok as my bodyguard, to infiltrate the high society of Craxon—and stir rebellion. For too long the planet had harbored the most vile slavers and condemned its victims to torment and death. Or worse.

It had to end.

A feminine cry distracted me from my darker musings and the insidious taste of the slavers' greed. I yanked on the reins. My catar whined at the sudden motion, spurring hard off the road. The movement stopped him in front of Pizon's pen in time to see the scaled alien raise his claws over a trembling figure.

"Orader," I called, intentionally using his type of species instead of his name. "What have you there?"

The bastard turned toward me with a grimace on his face. Before he could answer, however, whatever creature lay behind him began to crawl. I couldn't make it out well at first. But as it reached a hand toward me, the deepest parts of my brain began to fire. The haggard looking being on the dirt floor was female. She stared at me from eyes so brown they appeared like Xerion jewels. And her whispered word stopped my heart, "Human?"

I had no idea what this *human* word meant, and for some reason, my translator couldn't determine it. Yet the conviction in which she said it made me dismount. Brok stopped our convoy several paces ahead. We couldn't afford a delay, but neither would I turn away from this small female.

Dirt marred her face, hair, and all her skin that I could see. A gray garment covered her from shoulder to ankle, but it too was caked with dirt. She had delicate facial features: a tiny, upturned nose, pale pink lips, rounded ears, and soulful eyes. The last captured me, boring into my being as piercing as the blade at my back. I had taken several steps forward, standing just outside the plasti-shield, without knowing how I'd done it.

"What are you?" I said it to her, but Pizon answered. Out of all the slavers, I hated him most. He was unnecessarily cruel and enjoyed his job.

"She'sss a Terran. Very rare and fresssh." His mandibles clicked in a twisted snarl.

My stomach dropped, the morning's stew like poison inside me. I knew already I couldn't leave her to this bastard's hands. I turned to him, dragging him away from the female so she wouldn't overhear. "How much?"

"For you?" The clicking intensified. "Fifty drauma."

An obscene amount. I didn't have time for his games. I'd offer him the highest reasonable price and give him no quarter to argue. "Thirty-five." I unclipped a pouch from my belt, shook out the coins, and threw them at him. "I'll return in three spans to pick her up." It would take that long to drop off our couple to the ship, see them settled, and get back here. With the planet's suns not yet at their peak, we could achieve our goals well before darkness fell—and the frost turned biting.

Pizon clawed at the pouch. He measured its weight in his palm, before hissing, "Done."

"Good. I expect her to be ready when I return." I had to turn around, walk away. If I looked at this Terran female again, I would be tempted to take her now. I couldn't risk it with people relying on me to complete my mission. Newly rescued slaves were wild cards. Sometimes they fought, sometimes they ran, sometimes they cowered. It took time for them to trust us.

And time I didn't have.

Mounting my catar, I angled it toward the pen and stared down at Pizon. "She will be kept safe for me, or there will be consequences. Understand?"

"Of courssse, my Lord." The foul bastard inclined his mandibles at me. "Have I let you down before?"

He had in fact. Several times. Sending slaves half starved, or beaten, or both. Yet I had no choice.

Don't look at the female. Don't look at the female.

I steered my catar forward, pushing my heels gently into its side to prompt a steady pace. The heat of her gaze bore into my back. I knew it. Could feel the intensity of it along my spine.

Don't do it.

I cast a glance over my shoulder. The quickest of looks. And there she was. On the floor, dirty and small, staring at me.

My hearts clenched, like she'd reached her tiny hand inside my chest and squeezed. *No.* That couldn't be. I had to be imagining it. Too many solar days spent on this cursed planet had me dreaming of the impossible.

Pulling my gaze away, I urged my catar to a faster stride. Brok hadn't waited while I dallied at the slavers' pens, and I needed to catch up to my quarry. They were my responsibility. I had shirked it for too long in exchange for a lone female slave.

As I caught up to the carriage, I noticed Maena and Tallis drove in the front position while Brok had taken my place guarding the rear.

"What was that about?" he drew his catar to the right, allowing me room to fall in pace beside him.

I shook my head. "Just another rescue for us to tend to later."

Brok's eyes narrowed, the black rims bleeding into the silver hue that ringed around his pupil. "Catar shit." His hands tightened visibly on the reins. "You're shaken, Xelan. I may not have your abilities to sense emotion in others. And the void beckons inside me…" He sighed and followed the carriage at a steady pace while I rode beside him. "But I am still of your *Brather*. And I can tell."

My gut tightened. The void had claimed us both faster than expected. The second biological stage of all Rhonar males drove an endless sense of loss and emptiness. One that we would feel until death, if our mates were not found. And with the all but extinction of our females, that was an inevitable conclusion.

Only a lucky few find the mate bond in other males. My thoughts turned bitter. The warrior pairings were rare but our lone solace, a shining light in the darkness of our kind's painful existence. Yet I'd found no attraction toward my fellow warriors, and thus, no hope for a fated mate among them. The loss left me sour as the void beckoned me without a reprieve.

Yet, the void was no excuse for my treatment toward Brok. He was my closest friend, a warrior of my *Brather*. Not by blood but choice. An unbreakable bond forged from childhood. And I had lied to him. "Apologies, Brok."

"None needed. Just tell me what has you rattled." He turned his gaze ahead. No doubt allowing me the relief from his scrutiny.

But he wouldn't let this line of questioning go, and in truth, I didn't want to hide what I had encountered. "A girl. The slaver called her a Terran. She——"

The carriage jerked abruptly to a halt, forcing us to yank on our catars' reins. Brok and I both rode around on either side of the carriage to the front. Maena held onto Tallis' arm, her lavender skin paling to a dull gray. Tallis kept his gaze forward, elongated oval eyes turning wider in his plum colored faced. While his natural skin was darker than his wife's, it too paled. But he hung on to the reins with an expert grip. In front of the carriage a gorgoth snorted smoke and dug its massive claws into the dirt road. Its golden brown scales reflected the sunlight. Each of its two legs was more than half the length of our catars and its chest larger than our carriage.

Atop the beast sat Denthar Calth, one of the native Lords of Craxon, and our biggest obstacle in eliminating the slave trade on this planet. His close to unbreakable skin was a collection of gray scales, tougher than Rhonar steel. Four curved horns jutted from his naked skull. Animal hide covered his chest, waist, and thighs in the Craxion Elite fashion. A long cloak in deep crimson flowed behind him. He wore no shoes in the stirrups of his mount, showing his powerful hooves. Although the gorgoth outmatched our catars, Calth was shorter than Brok and me, but likely no less capable in a fight.

Brok's hand went to the hilt of his battle ax strapped behind him.

We had no time for this. Kicking my catar into motion, I skirted around the carriage and up to the gorgoth. It spat in my direction, but Calth reared back on the reins.

"Excuse my mount, dear Xelan." The honeyed words dropped from between Calth's thin lips. "It appears we're at an impasse."

"Not at all, Lord Calth." I inclined my head at him; although, I had rather bared my teeth. "We will veer off the road so that you may pass unheeded." Not giving him a chance to respond, I steered my catar into the dirt, motioning for the carriage to follow. Brok growled as we began to pass round the gorogth and the Craxion bastard. But otherwise, he said nothing. His hand did not stray from his ax.

"How accommodating of you," Calth called over his shoulder. "Such lovely manners for a foreigner."

"Of course." I tried not to choke on the words. While diplomacy led us to make gains in attaining our goal to liberate the planet, it still tasted sour on my tongue. As did the smug arrogance emanating from the Craxion. I nearly gagged on the emotion slipping past my empathic barriers.

"Oh, and Xelan." He turned his mount to look over the carriage at me as we retook the road behind him. "I will be having one of my gatherings soon. I shall send you an invitation."

My chest tightened, but I could let nothing show on my face. This was the final step we had been waiting for. Getting into one of the infamous Elite parties and attaining evidence of the atrocities committed would be the proof required to incite the rebels. It was the last ammunition we needed for true change to commence. "That is most gracious of you, Lord." I plastered on a smile, hoping it didn't look as forced as it felt. "I am honored."

"Indeed." He nodded, then whirled his beast around and trotted off. The dirt kicked up behind him, but I no longer cared even as it peppered the back of the carriage.

"At last." I grinned, genuinely this time, at my companions. "We have our chance."

Chapter 3

AVA

Royal blue. I shut my eyes attempting to capture the color. As the man—well, male anyway—had come closer to the shielding, the fishbowl effect had lessened, and I could see…him. I'd never been so captivated by anyone before, as if turning away would somehow cause physical pain. His skin was a unique shade between copper and bronze with a tougher look to it than a human's. But he appeared human, or at least humanoid, with a strong, angular jaw, and thick brows. His shoulders were broad and covered in leather-like armor that I'd only read about in fantasy books. The armor didn't cover his arms, but tattoos of swirling designs did, except they seemed to be made of metal instead of black ink.

Everything about him was so different…alien, and yet, comforting and familiar. *How?*

I didn't have long to contemplate. He had stared at me for only a heartbeat, after I whispered, "human," to him. I didn't know if I was answering his question about my species or asking if he was like me. It had just slipped out. But before I could say more, he'd turned and said something to the bug-man. Then, he'd left. I'd crawled after him, coming right up to the plastic wall. But he didn't turn back.

My hope went with him.

Now, the bug-man yanked on my hair. "Up, up, Terran." I grasped at his lobster claw, but he only tugged me harder. Rising to my full height, he wrenched my head back. "You must be fresssh for the Rhonar massster. Yesss. He paysss good money for you."

I glanced back toward the plastic walls. Had the alien male bought me? If so, then why did he leave me here? With no answers, a new fear gripped me. I had reacted so strangely to his presence. Did he have some type of mind control ability? Panic crawled up my throat.

I couldn't stay here. I had to get free.

Twisting in the bug-man's hold, I kicked at his midsection. He let out a surprised hiss and loosened his grip. I tore free and headed toward the wall. It had to have an exit. Somewhere. Racing around and around, I ran my hands along the translucent fishbowl. It was as hard as I'd imagined with no indentation in sight.

"No," I cried as the bug-man chased after me. I chanced a peek behind me to find his hulking form moving far faster than I would have guessed from his size. It was also why I didn't see the creature in front of me until it was too late. My face smacked into something like steel. I groaned, pulling my head away and rubbing my nose. Tears sprang to my eyes. I blinked them away, trying to see through the pain.

I wished I hadn't…again.

Standing in front of me was a creature that made bug-man look tame. Gray scales covered its body. Its hands were tipped with claws, and it had hooves for feet. It wore a crimson cloak and animal hide. Four long curved horns stuck out from its bald scalp. Thin lips spread into a sardonic smile while a coal-black gaze pierced through me.

I shivered, then froze like prey caught in a trap. My mouth widened to an O shape and a choked sound came forth.

"What have we here?" The gray beast said. "So lovely."

Dread pooled in my stomach. His expression changed from one of disdain to an interest recognizable anywhere, in any galaxy—desire. I screamed, "Demon!"

The logical part of my brain told me this was another alien, not a devil. But my lizard brain cried out for me to run. Far and fast. That a monster would devour me. And that primal part was in full control. I turned to flee, but not before bug-man came up behind me and captured his claws around my shoulders.

"She's a feisty one, hmm?" The gray beast bent his head and sniffed along my cheek. "I like that."

"Yesss, my Lord," the bug-man said. "I am fortunate to sssell her already."

The monster's lust-filled face changed to anger in an instant, his ridged brow sinking into a scowl. He stared over my head at the bug-man. "And who has purchased her?"

The bug-man's hissing words grated my ears. "Xelan of the Rhonar warriorsss."

"Ah, I see." The gray beast smiled down at me again. From the inside of his cloak, he extracted a device. I squinted at the cylindrical object in his claws. Shaped like a sword hilt with no blade, it bore indentations at its base. "You may borrow this to make her more pliable. After all, I would not like my new friend to have a recalcitrant slave." A cold grin warped his lips as he put his face closer to mine. "The Rhonar are far too," he nicked my chin, "soft."

Blood pooled where his claw cut me, but I barely felt it. I blamed shock and prayed silently for the respite it offered.

"Thank you, my Lord." The bug-man let one claw fall away from my arm to take the offered device. "I ssshall ussse it well."

"Do so, Pixon. And see to it that her new master knows who helped him." He readjusted his cloak with a flourish and spun on his hooves. Over his shoulder he called back, "I would have his thanks."

"Of course, Lord Calth." The bug-man bowed. "It shall be so."

A slit appeared in the plastic wall, opening a doorway wide enough for the gray beast to walk through. Then, it sealed behind him and the seam disappeared. "Now, Terran…" The bug-man dragged me toward the center and through the curved doorway where I first began this sickening nightmare. He flung me toward the cage, but not in it. Pressing an indentation in the cylindrical device, I stared in horror as the thing sprung to life. Long tendrils of electricity shot out like living tentacles. They spun and danced, spitting sparks along the dirt floor. "It is time for you to learn your place."

I couldn't even find the courage to scream.

XELAN

Everything took too long. Our luck hadn't lasted after the invitation from that Craxion bastard brought us one step closer to our goals. The carriage wheel broke again, our companions were late to the meeting point, and our poor charge started to have birthing pains before we made it to the ship. The only bright spot was that it had been a false alarm, and she had not actually begun to give birth. Or so Miach, our healer, assured me.

Once the rescues were safely aboard the ship, Miach had wanted us to stay for a while and give the history of anything we knew about the rescues, especially the woman with child. I'd grumbled, and Brok had remained silent. While I usually relished the chance to converse with more of my fellow Rhonar warriors, today my mind was occupied with a small Terran slave.

"Xelan," Miach had chided. "What has you so twisted up?"

I'd ignored his question and dove into the fastest report ever given. Not that we knew much about our charges, only that we'd found them huddled outside of an inn. They'd claimed to be workers, but it was clear from their clothes and demeanor they'd been outcast slaves. Too much for their owners to feed, but not worth enough under the Craxion slave trade to be brought to market for resale.

I conveyed all of this as quickly as I could, eager to regain the road.

"I see," Miach said and stepped closer into my space. It pushed the insistent feel of his curiosity past my empathic shields. Rhonar males might have most of their emotions suppressed but his inquisitive nature sure wasn't.

"Healer," I used his title in a barely restrained growl, "step back." I narrowed my eyes, knowing full well what he attempted. Miach's ability allowed him to see into others. It made him an excellent healer as he could view any ailment or injury within a person's body if he were physically close enough to them. But with our kind, he also sensed other things. Not emotions like I did, but he described it as a *knowing*. A sense of picking out what was wrong with a person.

I hated his perceptive skill almost as much as my empathic ability.

"Sorry." He held up his hands in surrender.

I'd had all I could take after that. Saluting our brathers' health as a goodbye, our company headed off ship and back to the road. Tallis and Maena guided the empty carriage while Brok and I followed behind. Craxon's suns sat much lower in the sky than I'd intended for our return trip, souring my mood.

"Want to tell me what that was all about?" Brok broke the heavy silence.

I sighed. "Not particularly."

He shrugged and allowed the silence to reclaim us. We stayed that way for the majority of the journey. But as behind schedule as we were, I found the pace set by our Kinsian attendants too slow to bear. I angled my catar around the carriage to retake the lead and kicked us into a quicker step. Not one of my companions said a word about it.

I was thankful, for I had no explanation for the dread that had claimed me. Yes, the trip to meet with our Rhonar brathers was always a risk, and the mishaps with the carriage didn't help this time, but it had still been successful. So why did my gut churn? I had no answer, but feelings that broke through the void eating at my existence were not to be ignored.

It was no surprise when Brok rounded the carriage and moved his catar into pace beside mine a short time later.

"You're agitated," he said simply.

I didn't confirm nor deny it. He was right, of course. But with no answers for the emotion that managed to creep past the void, what could I say?

"You should call for a florin." With that, he fell into pace behind the carriage, once more guarding our rear.

That was not happening. As much as those furry little creatures helped us, I didn't need one rifling around my empathic shields. Florins were inter-dimensional beings that traveled the planes of existence as easily as a space cruiser across the cosmos. They had discovered Rhonar warriors when we were at our lowest point. After the last war, a biological weapon constructed by our greatest enemy killed our females and sent us into the far reaches of space in search of our lost colonies. And our only chance at survival. We had been explorers once, and necessity made us explorers again.

The florins had been fascinated by our biological anomalies, a curse that only our mates could fix. Without them, we were doomed to the hunger and then, the void; our emotions repressed by each state. With their empathic abilities, the florins offered to lend us aid. Where I could sense the emotions of others, the florins could not only feel others' emotions, they could push emotions onto others. They allowed us to feel and gave us relief from our constant torment.

But for me...

The sensations felt odd, off, like dripping ice between my eyes. It was *not* pleasant. And I felt enough from everyone else. I didn't need to compound that with the florins' unique gift.

"Although, they might help me understand—"

I didn't finish the thought aloud before a wave of pain rushed at me. My empathic shields couldn't handle the overload, and I dropped off my catar. Maena screamed, and Tallis jerked the reins. The catars whined in protest. Brok rounded to the front while I struggled to regulate the pain.

"What is it?" He slid from his catar and knelt beside me.

"Pain," I hissed through my teeth.

His palm rested against my shoulder, desperation likely causing his fingers to clench at the muscle there. "How can I help?"

I couldn't answer. Slowly, very slowly, my shields thickened to block the intensity of the agony battering against them. I rose to my feet and placed my hand atop his that was still gripping my shoulder. "I'm well, Brokdar."

His pinched features said that he was not convinced, but he released me and stepped back. Having spent so much time in each other's company, he knew that proximity made it harder for me to control my internal shielding.

I didn't waste more time in locating the source of the pain. "Down the hill to our right." I jerked my chin in that direction. "The slave pens."

Brok followed where I indicated. "Why?"

I knew what he was asking. For all our rotations on this planet, all the slaves we had discreetly freed, I'd never been so affected by emotions as to knock me from my catar. I shrugged, not knowing what to say about it.

Without more words, we both regained our catars and headed toward the slave pens. It didn't take long before we spotted the source of the painful wave—Pizon's pen. Huddled in the corner was the small Terran female. As my gaze landed on the angry red welts across her back and the torn remains of her dull gray garment, an emotional avalanche crashed on me.

It had been long, so long since I'd felt anything. And now, my senses had been overloaded to the brink in one short day.

But this? This was the pinnacle. And Celestia help whoever crossed my path.

Chapter 4

XELAN

EVERY MUSCLE IN MY BODY TENSED TIGHTER THAN A wire, ready to snap. *Rage.* The sensation coated the fabric of my being like Syconian oil, blocking out the void that ate at my existence. How long had it been since I felt such a deep emotion? And two in one day? Unheard of. But seeing this small Terran female in pain, her back marred with vicious wounds, had set my kedara on fire. My life's blood burned through me, and the katra symbols on my arms and shoulders glowed red.

"Pizon," I bellowed his name, dangerously close to losing control. "What in the crex have you done?"

The scaly bastard had the gall to raise his mandibles in his version of a smile. "I have broken her in for you, my Lord. Yesss, I have."

That was all I needed to hear. I launched at him so hard, we bounced as his body hit the dirt under mine.

Without thought, I pounded fist after fist upon him. My katra continued to glow as his blood splattered on my arms and chest, the greenish tinge of it a strange contrast. Yet, I couldn't stop, nor even slow. A madness drove me on.

"You dared," I squeezed through a clenched jaw, "harm her?"

"Ssstop," the bastard hissed as his left jaw bone cracked.

It didn't slow my attack. Only solid arms locking around my chest caused any pause. "Calm yourself," Brok said stoically by my ear. "You can't help the female this way."

That did it.

I eased off my foe. Brok released me to rise to my feet. I looked down at the bloody mess I'd caused without remorse. "What did you use?"

The wounds on the female's back were like none I'd seen before. If we were to heal her, we'd need to know the cause.

"L-Lord Cal-th," he stuttered past his broken mandible. "G-gave me thisss." He held up a rod about the length of my forearm.

Grabbing it from him, I held the device to the light. On the side, several indentations appeared. I pressed the first one, and sparks flared from the end. As I pushed at the second spot, the sparks elongated into ropes of electricity. The third turned the energy higher.

My hand vibrated, from anger or the device, I couldn't tell. Likely both. I removed my fingers to turn off the torture instrument and handed it to Brok. "Tie my catar to the rear and have Maena meet me inside the carriage. I'll need her help in tending to the female."

Brok inclined his head, leaving to carry out my orders.

I turned to the bastard who still laid on the ground. "If you ever injure anyone, slave or no, in this manner or any other again," the katra on my arms continued to glow like a warning light to my words, "I will leave you in pieces." A minor sense of satisfaction ran through me as he flinched. I didn't even blink at the newest emotion. "Do you understand?"

"Yesss, Lord." He ducked his head.

I had no more words to waste on him. As to Lord Calth, that would be dealt with in time. I longed to make him pay for all the pain he had caused on this cursed planet, but in this instance, I didn't want justice. I wanted revenge. I wanted to see him bleed. And that I could feel such hatred confused me.

I stared at the female. Her eyes were closed and her breathing was shallow. I had to hurry.

She didn't stir when I reached under her to lift her like a babe to my chest. Her head lolled forward, loose strands of her hair grazing my arm. My katra at last turned to its normal metallic shade, but a slight glow still caused light to fall on her face. Even through the pained circles around her eyes, she was beautiful. I tried not to stare.

The female was injured, and I had to be careful where I rested my hands beneath her so as not to disturb her wounds.

With care, I carried her to the carriage. Once inside, Maena sprang into action. Her lavender palm rested gently on the female's forehead. "I don't know her species normal body temperature, but she feels icy to the touch, and she shakes."

I hadn't noticed past the emotions ravaging through me, but Maena was correct. The small female in my arms was shaking herself apart. "What can we do?"

"We have to keep her warm without covering her back. Those wounds are concerning, and I dare not put anything on them here. I have no medical bandage." My sweet Kinsian attendant wrung her hands together. Maena and Tallis had been one of our earliest rescues. Captured by slavers while on holiday, they suffered through a long transport before arriving on Craxon. Half-starved and terrified, they still had an undeniable light in their eyes. Brok and I had spotted them in the pens. When we bought them and told them they were free, they refused to leave our service and begged instead to help with our cause. Now, they were our most trusted companions.

Although the little female remained unconscious, her body radiated pain and cold. "How do we warm her if she cannot be covered?"

"Remove your armor, lean back, and pull her tight against your chest. One arm at her hips and the other above her shoulder like you did when you carried her." Maena angled her body to block the carriage door. "Your kind run hot, and I will sit this way to block any stray drafts from the door."

I placed the female on the carriage bench on her side so I could strip off my armor as directed. "Will that be enough?" The churning sensation in my gut returned, replacing all remnants of anger.

"It will have to be." Maena brushed the female's hair from her face, running her long double-knuckled fingers through the strands. "It's all we can do for now."

As I dropped my armor to the carriage floor and pulled the female once more to my chest, she began to stir. If she awoke now, she'd feel all the pain, and she might struggle in my grip. I could not allow that.

"Florin!" I called, looking upward more out of habit than necessity since the doorways between dimensions existed all around us. "Hear me."

The florins promised they would aid us whenever we had need of them. In exchange, they could siphon some of our energy that they required to survive. But the call to them was not foolproof, depending on whether one of their kind was in range of hearing us. The knowledge of inter-dimensional travel was not of interest to the Rhonar since we didn't possess the capabilities to pass through the planes, but in truth, I understood even less of it. I only knew that sometimes a florin would appear at our call, and sometimes it would not. I prayed this time I'd be heard.

I didn't have long to wait. As the female blinked up at me, a florin as blue as a lyzanthia bloom appeared at my feet.

"What? No!" The female's frightened cry pierced through me, and she began to thrash as I'd feared.

"Hush now, child." Maena tried to soothe her, but the female continued to scream.

Her gaze tracked around the carriage. "Let me go!"

"Quickly," I said to the florin. It angled its head to the side as if in question. "Push this female to be at ease and sleep."

The florin jumped on the bench beside us and began to coo. The soft purring sound seemed to have the desired effect. The female's eyelids fluttered once, twice, and then closed. Slowly her body relaxed, resting against mine. Her breathing evened and a soft snore began.

My double hearts beat regularly now too.

"Thank you." I inclined my head toward the florin. This one had a furry blue body with white on its stomach and paws, a trademark of their kind, and lighter blue around its eyes and head. Its large triangular ears stood in opposition to its tiny face. White fur ran across its muzzle. Three bushy tails helped him to balance. Those tails now thumped in recognition of my words.

Some of the florin spoke to us in words, while others simply let their actions speak for them. It appeared this one was the latter. It jumped on my shoulder, staring into my eyes. I nodded, letting him know the exchange was agreed upon. A tiny paw touched my temple, and a tug began at the spot. Slowly a small amount of energy drained from me.

When the florin had finished, he patted my temple and popped out of our dimension.

Relief flowed through me as the female continued to sleep on my chest. Maena examined the wounds on her back as we began the trek, gently prodding the skin. It wasn't far to our makeshift home, although it could hardly be called "home" in a place such as this. Yet, it served our purposes, and our Kinsian couple did their best to make it feel inviting. I hoped that when the female felt better, she would like it.

Wait. Why does that matter?

The errant thought appeared, unwelcome and accompanied by a nagging worry. I glanced at the female. Her hair tickled my chin where the top of her head rested. Her exposed shoulder bore an array of mottled bruises. The welts on her back were raised and raw, sending a fresh rush of anger clawing its way through my ribs. These conflicting emotions zapped at the void inside me, filling it with swirls of… something.

I didn't know what to make of it all. Why now was I feeling again?

The simplest answer was not worth examining. It couldn't be true. Our female population had been decimated in the last war, battles that haunted me even several orbits later, and although some of my brathers held hope in finding our lost colonies of the past, I did not. Long before the wars, our ancestors had set forth into the universe. But that was over eighteen thousand orbits ago. The odds of finding our descendants in the vastness of the universe, after all that time, were impossible. Only a fool entertained the impossible. And I was no fool. Not anymore.

"Sir," Maena's soft voice and gentle hand on my arm roused me from my musings.

"I've told you to call me Xelan." I chided.

She smiled. "I know, but when we're out or around others, Tallis and I must present as the dutiful slaves." Her fingers glided along the female's skin with infinite care. "We can never be too careful."

"You're right." I sighed, the air caressing the female's dark hair. "I'm just…"

"On edge," she provided.

The clawing sensation returned, creeping up my neck. It wasn't anger this time, but it left me…unsettled. "I suppose."

"That's not like you." Maena eyed me and clearly waited for a response. When I didn't reply, she said, "You know, this female resembles your kind."

I balked at the suggestion. Maena and Tallis knew the history of the Rhonar. She knew that others of my brathers searched, even now, endlessly for the chance, the smallest of chances, to find our descendants. I would not give them false hope. I'd never look to Celestia or any other deity or fate of the cosmos for hope again.

"It's a vague similarity at best." It was true. The female in my arms had some matches, but so did many creatures throughout the galaxies. Two eyes were framed by thick eyelashes that fanned against her cheeks. A small, delicate nose rested at the center of her face. Her lips were pink and lush, perfect for taking, claiming in a passionate…

My blood churned, an answering response sweeping my body as I gazed at the face of the lovely female.

Maena drew my attention, a knowing lavender finger wagged under my nose. "I think it's more than that." Her expression held understanding as our eyes met. "But we shall see when she is well again."

I sobered at that. While I might not yet understand why these emotions—and needs—were growing inside me, I did know one thing for certain. I wanted this female whole and healthy, to see her live and thrive. She might yet be a stranger, but her safety and happiness were more vital to me than all other concerns. And why that might have been, well, only the stars knew.

Chapter 5

AVA

I was caught in a dream. Snippets flashed behind my sleeping eyes that told a strange story. Electrified whips, searing pain, darkness, and then, a voice called to me. Deep and soothing, it felt like a balm to my troubled mind.

More darkness followed.

Out of the depths, I stirred and rose to almost wakefulness. I reached and grabbed for it, trying to stay conscious. A furry blue creature appeared. It looked like a plushie toy that a child dreamed up, part rabbit, corgi dog, and three-tailed fox mixed together in one being. And blue, so very blue. It cooed at me, and darkness took me again.

The images disappeared, but my other senses grew attuned to my environment. I heard the deep, soothing voice talking with a higher-pitched one. Fingers prodded my back gently. A hard, warm pillow laid under my body. The scent of rich chocolate filled my nose. Not the cheap mass-produced kind either, but the aroma you'd smell in the shop of a master chocolatier. I breathed it in. Then, I was floating. Light hit my closed lids, but my eyes refused to open. Steps, like the sound of heavy boots on a solid surface, echoed around me.

I caught fragmented words from hushed but agitated voices. "Water. Clean cloth. Hurry."

I landed on a soft cloud and strong hands turned me onto my stomach. Shuffling and clanging noises reached my ears. Then, an odd aroma hit me, and darkness came a final time.

Everything went still afterward. I knew nothing, felt nothing as I stayed suspended in that dark place. When I could at last open my eyes once more and arouse to full consciousness, I had no comprehension of my surroundings.

Warm orange light filtered through white billowing curtains, and a cool breeze made them move like dancing phantoms. A glowing pink fire emanated heat from a large stone hearth. As my gaze wandered, I caught sight of the corner post of the bed where I laid. It was like no material I'd ever seen, black as night and smoother than marble. Beyond it, in a chair that seemed to be made of the same substance as the bedpost, sat a man. I squinted to make him out better.

Even seated, he appeared huge. His elbows rested on his thighs, the latter as large as tree trunks. He held his head in his hands as if all the world's weight sat on his hunched shoulders. His legs and chest were covered in a leather-like material with the top patterned in some type of armor. His arms were bare of clothing but held intricate tattoos that appeared metallic. Dark brown hair flowed backward from his proud forehead to his ears.

I wanted to see his face.

The thought gripped me so hard, as if a vise had squeezed inside my chest. I urged my chapped and dried lips to make a sound, any sound. What came forth was a quiet whimper.

It was enough.

The man inclined his head toward me. My breathing stopped. Royal blue eyes stared into mine with such a force and intensity, I would have fallen over, if I weren't lying down. I knew those eyes. I had seen them before, but where?

I sucked in a breath, choking on it as my throat tightened.

The cage.

Everything hit me hard, the weight of memories slamming into my skull. My body shook, and I couldn't stop the tears that sprang forward.

The male—not a man at all for I now recognized him as the alien who "bought" me—rose to his feet. His brows drew low, and he reached for something out of my view. I stiffened, bracing for whatever was to come. He crouched beside the bed, his head still inches above mine.

"Drink this," he said and brought a Medieval-looking and elaborately carved goblet to my lips. "It's water."

I didn't reply. And I didn't drink.

Fire rose within me, a burning fury that started in the pit of my stomach and brushed along every fiber of my being. I blinked away the tears. How dare this bastard think he could own me, buy me, like I was nothing more than an object. I kept my abused lips firmly closed.

He sighed, and it reverberated along my spine, quenching the angry fire within. Why should that disappointed sound affect me?

"Look," he said, crouching even lower so I could see inside the goblet. "I promise it's water, and you need it." He took a sip and swallowed, then showed me inside again. "See?"

I peered into it. It looked like water, but how was I to know? I had no reason to trust an alien that would buy another living, breathing being. Even if he was striking, mesmerizing. I was staring into his eyes again, drowning in those endless blue pools. The anger that had risen so fast was equally snuffed out by his sighs and his gaze. By blue, infinite blue.

I shook my head to clear it and looked pointedly away from him.

He sighed again, and I fought the effects of that sound. "I know you have no reason to trust me." Inching closer, his warm breath fanned the side of my neck. I had to keep my face planted in the bedsheets. I'd be lost otherwise. "But please, just drink. You were badly hurt, and you've slept for two days. You need to drink."

That got my attention.

Two days? What happened? I remembered the cage, the bug-man, this alien's royal blue eyes, and then…my mind blanked as if to protect itself. The flashes I'd gotten in my dream state were lost or muddled. Begrudgingly, I turned to face him.

I didn't speak. I wouldn't give him that much. I kept my gaze on the goblet, silently agreeing to drink.

He must have gotten my message as he tilted the rim to my lips. Once the water touched my tongue, I realized how badly I needed it and gulped it down.

"Not too fast." He inched it away. I groaned. "You can have more, but slowly. We don't want you getting sick."

I furrowed my brow. His words were reasonable. I hated them nonetheless. He was my captor now. I couldn't trust him, especially not with the strange reactions I kept having around him. Was he using a mind trick? I had to stay on guard.

He gently tipped the goblet toward me once more and continued talking as I drank slower this time. "My name is Xelan. I'm a Rhonar warrior. And you are safe here." I huffed at that, but he didn't seem put off by my response. When I had my fill, he put the water aside. "I understand your mistrust. But know no harm will come to you, I promise you this." He paused as if thinking on his words. "I won't allow you to suffer ever again."

The conviction with which he said this pulled me in like a magnet, despite my better judgment. I peered at his thick brows, his angular jaw. I didn't meet his eyes, but I could feel his intense gaze on me. My breathing sped up as did my heart rate. I heard his harsh intake of air. Was I somehow having the same effect on him? That would be a twist, but I had no way of knowing for sure. *And what would it matter anyway?* I was a prisoner, a slave. He bought me. That's all I knew. And I had to find a way to escape.

As if reading my thoughts, he said, "I'm sure you're worried about what happened. But you don't need to be. You aren't a prisoner here. As soon as we can make arrangements, as soon as you're healed, you'll be free."

I didn't believe that for a minute. And healed? I hadn't noticed it until now, but my body did feel sluggish and sore, like I'd been through a battle. I knew the ship I was on had been attacked, and I had been abducted. I remembered that horrible fishbowl cage, the weird bug-man, and…

The image of a giant gray devil flashed before my eyes.

I cried out.

"Are you in pain?" The alien male, this Xelan, rested his hands on my shoulders, angling his body in front of me and forcing my gaze to his. "Please tell me. I want to help you."

His pleading eyes touched something deep inside me. It washed away the terrifying memory of that beast, but it couldn't make me forget what came after. The bug-man had cornered me inside and taken out a whip with lashes of pure electricity. I remembered the horrible sizzling of it as it landed across my back. I must have lost consciousness quickly as the rest was lost in a fog.

The trauma of it, however, remained. Yet, I wasn't feeling pain, not as much as I should. I patted my back where I could reach while remaining lying on my stomach. Puckered skin met my fingertips in spots, but it didn't hurt. I let my hand flop to my side. Although I didn't trust the male in front of me, I also didn't have any inclination to move. It had to be the result of my injuries, even if I didn't feel the pain from them.

His eyes had tracked where my hands had skimmed along my back. His voice was gruff as he said, "Maena, one of my attendants and a friend, treated you." He rose, palms out in front of him, showing me his movements. "I'm going to cover you with the sheet that's by your feet. Yes?"

I nodded, a concession to be sure, but I wanted my back covered. Lying on my stomach, my injured back exposed, felt too vulnerable. A sheet wouldn't provide much protection. Still, it was better than nothing.

The sheet glided over me, covering me from the neck down. Then, he took the same spot as before, crouching by my head. "Are you comfortable?"

I snorted.

He laughed at that, the sound rusty as if he hadn't done it often. Yet, it warmed me more than the strange pink fire or the sheet over me. I cursed the weakness.

"I apologize." He scrubbed a hand down his face, an all too human gesture that left me unnerved. "That was a foolish question." Rising, he went to the fire, stoking the flames higher in the hearth. It shot pink sparks over the polished stones and created a beautiful display.

I sighed. I didn't want to enjoy anything about my situation, not even the beauty of the fire. And I certainly did not want to feel any type of warmth toward my captor. Yet, there I laid, wounds tended, thirst quenched, and senses captivated by pink flames…and a blue-eyed alien.

Xelan, as I now started to think of him by name, turned back to me. He grabbed a cushion from a cabinet I hadn't noticed earlier and tossed it on the floor. The metallic tattoos on his arms glowed pink from the firelight. He sat on the cushion, allowing his head to be level with mine once more. He could have taken the chair again. He didn't have to keep our faces at eye level, but he did.

It could be an act, a ploy to get me to trust him. Yet, my intuition told me that wasn't the case. So, when he began to talk again, I listened with an open mind. Well, as open as I could manage anyway.

"My brather, Brok, and I have been on this planet for many cycles. I'm not sure how your people calculate time, but we've seen all of Craxon's seasons." He waved toward the open window. "That's the planet you're on, Craxon," he added. "And well, it's been," he peered into the fire for a heart-beat before facing me again, "challenging."

Another quiet moment passed before he continued, "We've come here to help the rebellion, but we're doing it undercover, posing as part of the ruling class. Slavery is abhorrent to us and our code of honor, and while we don't make it a rule to interfere with other cultures, we do, at times, make exceptions." He grinned, and the expression made him look years younger. Then, his smile fell. "We have many reasons to aid those who would rise against slavery and the atrocities of it."

I held my breath. I wanted desperately to believe him. He'd shown me kindness since I'd awoken, but it could be a trick. Some game he was playing, right?

"When I saw you in that pen, I had a strong urge to help you." He rested his left hand on the bed beside me, his fingers outstretched to stroke the ends of my hair. "I fought the impulse. We had two other people in our carriage. We had to get them to our brathers, so they could receive medical attention and gain passage off this accursed planet." His voice lowered to a whisper. "If I had known what would happen, I would never have left you."

The air whooshed from my lungs. Our eyes locked, and for long seconds, neither of us moved. Then, the fire crackled loudly, and the spell between us broke.

He jerked his hand away. "I'm…" Turning his palm over, he stared at his fingers as if fascinated by them. "I'm glad that you're healing. Maena will come to check on you. The herbal remedy she used is helping, but she'll want to take a look herself." His fingers curled into a fist, and he placed it behind his back. "Before I leave you to rest, will you tell me your name?"

A war took place inside me. My heart—and my body— reached for him, an undeniable attraction like a magnetic charge; yet the logical side, my brain told me that it could still be an elaborate deception. That he wanted something from me. I couldn't decide which was right, and so I remained quiet.

He rose without another word and headed for the door.

"Ava." I cleared my throat, voice scratchy from disuse. "Ava May Kouris."

I might not have known if I could trust him, but I had to start somewhere if I was going to gain my freedom.

Xelan glanced over his shoulder, gifting me with a wide, genuine smile. "Aaaava," he said, elongating the "A" like a musical note. Then, his expression changed, his eyes going impossibly round and his jaw clenching tight enough to crack. He groaned through his gritted teeth, then his eyes rolled up into his head, and he collapsed with a deafening crash.

Chapter 6

XELAN

SAO-SAO BIRDS. SAO-SAO BIRDS FLEW OVERHEAD. THEIR twitters and caws called to each other, bright green feathered wings gliding on mild winds. "Xelan, do you see them? Do you see the sao-sao birds?" The soft feminine voice was familiar, but it had been long, so long since I'd last heard it. I tried to discover the source of the voice, but I couldn't see its owner. Thick clouds surrounded me as if I had been caught in a fog. "Over here!" A hand waved in the distance beyond the mist, but as I squinted and ran toward it, it moved further away.

She was running.

"Calzara, wait!" I could see her now, a faint outline on the horizon. I cut through the fog barehanded, willing it to disperse. She was sprinting fast, heading toward the water, the black waters where I could not follow. "No! Please." The dense vapors clogged my throat and stung my eyes, but she was running, still running. I begged and pleaded for her to stop.

But I knew she would not.

"I can't, my dear brather." Her voice floated back to me. As her body moved forward into the churning dark waves, her words remained behind. "I'm already gone."

I awoke with a pained roar. It tore from my twin hearts as if the agony of it was fresh.

"Xelan? Xelan?" Another female called to me. *Who is she?* A fragrance as sweet as a Yalian flower in bloom tickled my nose. And instinctively I knew, it was her. My eyes opened. "Ava."

I laid on the floor, flat on my back. My senses were fragmented and jumbled. Emotions, so many emotions churned through me, filling the void, stuffing it to overflowing. I'd never felt so much, so quickly. It was too much. I couldn't get my shields through the stifling feelings as they were not external. They were mine. They were *all* mine.

"Are you all right?" The female, Ava, knelt beside me.

I laid a fist against my sternum, willing my pounding double hearts to slow. Only one thing could cause such turmoil. But I would not utter the thought aloud for even the slightest chance I was wrong.

I had to get away fast.

"Yes." I ground between clenched teeth. How in the name of Celestia did I manage these emotions? I rose to my feet slowly and pointed to the bed. I didn't dare touch her. "You should get back in bed."

She crossed her arms over her breasts, her bare breasts. Maena had stripped Ava's clothes off to better tend to her back. Her nudity hadn't been a problem while she was recuperating. She had spent that time lying on her stomach with her lower half covered by blankets. But now, I struggled to ignore her naked body. It was… perfect. *She* was perfect.

However, she appeared unaware of her current state. "Well, excuse me for trying to help."

I cast my gaze to the floor, waiting for her to return to the bed. I needed distance. *Now*. My blood rose hot and heavy as if emphasizing my suspicions. I'd seen beautiful females before, been with them intimately. The results had been born of physical desire, nothing more. Although I made certain my partners enjoyed it. The need to please a partner in bed was biologically ingrained in all Rhonar males. It was only the hunger or the void that denied any deeper connection. Unless, it was…

No, I wouldn't think it. Not yet. Not until I was sure.

I had to have space, distance to uncover the truth. Yet I couldn't leave her unattended. "I appreciate it." I tried for a milder tone. "But you're uh…you should stay covered."

That seemed to do the trick. Although I kept my eyes averted, I heard her squeak and shuffle onto the bed.

"Why am I naked?" Her tone carried both anger and fear. The feelings radiated from her and pummeled my senses.

"Your injuries needed tending." Drav it, I had to go. Between her emotions hitting me like a battering ram and my newly acquired feelings spinning like a Gorgonian windstorm, I had little control. Not to mention my cock was stiffening to a degree that would soon be a problem. I snorted at the damn thing, attempting to think of anything beyond the gorgeous naked female before me. What was I talking about? Her back, crex. "Uh, Maena took care of it."

"Yeah, whatever." Her huff spoke volumes. "I want my clothes back."

"And you'll get them," I said rougher than I intended, "when you're healed."

"No. I want them now."

I spun on my heel, glaring at her. A mistake as more emotions rushed through the fragments of my shielding. Her floral scent hit my nose again, spiking my arousal. It set my nerves aflame. "You want the tattered remains we found you in? Is that what you want?"

She rose to her knees on the bed. The sheet clutched tightly to her chest. "I want what's mine."

"You have nothing that's yours now." A cacophony of feeling ate at my insides. I had to get out of this room and under control. "The inhabitants will see you as nothing but a slave. Until we can arrange your freedom, you are stuck here. And you will not put my people in danger. You will act the part. Understand?"

Her eyes, those Xerion jewel-toned brown eyes, shot daggers at me. "A slave? You want me to act like a slave?"

"Yes," I hissed. "For now, that's what you are." Oh drav. I stepped right into a steaming pile of catar dung with that remark. My katra began to glow, my arms turning a bright red amid the pink firelight.

Ava's chest rose and fell beneath the sheet, her lush breasts moving under the fabric. Her cheeks turned an enticing rose hue. The fist against her chest held a death grip on the thin material. She had been beautiful before, but in her anger, she was like an avenging goddess.

The urge to kiss her until that heated rage turned to passion nearly undid me. I took a full step toward her before her fierce stare changed. Her bottom lip trembled and her eyes grew glassy.

"Crex me," I cursed. I whirled away and headed for the exit. "Rest. Maena will be here soon to check on you." With that, I escaped into the hall, closing the door firmly behind me.

I needed to conquer this madness, to master these emotions. And to get a hold on this gnawing, biting lust.

I needed to be alone. Calling forth a single word that all my companions would understand, I yelled, "Isolation." It didn't matter who of them heard. They would let the others know. My empathic gift was all too often a curse, and when my shields were at their lowest, Brok, Maena, and Tallis, all knew what I needed.

Solitude.

As I headed for the basement that housed the isolation chamber, my gut churned. Had I imagined it all?

Ava was a great beauty with her long black hair and sparkling eyes. Although she was small, much more so than me, she had generous curves that a male could easily imagine filling his palms. I had needed to keep her warm during the night when Craxon's frost season turned dangerously cold. On the first evening, while she still laid unconscious, she had nearly shook herself off the bed. Yet we couldn't cover her upper body with anything more than a sheet with her back so injured. Maena advised holding her as I had in the carriage, but I didn't want to put the poor female's modesty at risk, nor incur her wrath if she awoke. So, we devised a plan.

We'd placed Ava on her stomach with her legs and backside covered by several thick blankets. Then, I laid beside her as close as I dared to give her my body heat. Between that and stoking the fire in the hearth every few hours, it managed to keep her temperature even. It wasn't a perfect solution, but it kept her from freezing. If we'd been able to bring our tech to this draving planet besides the isolation chamber that we hid in the basement, or to take the tiny female to our ship, none of this would have been an issue. But, with Craxon not being as technologically advanced and us trying to blend in, and our ship currently off tending to our last rescues, we made do with what we had. Even now, Maena was preparing a new medicine that, when ready, would heal Ava's wounds rapidly.

That at least was a relief. I dreaded having to tell Ava about how we'd kept her warm. "And how you'll need to do so again, except she'll be awake this time," I mumbled to the empty basement. I knew already the fiery female wouldn't take it well, especially after our last interaction.

I sighed. Sleeping beside her hadn't felt intimate at the time. I'd only desired to help her, but perhaps I'd been lying to myself. I stripped off my chest armor, baring my skin to the chill room. It didn't bother me as my blood continued to run hotter than it ever had. I climbed into the isolation chamber, turning the settings to release me before night fell. Whether I was ready or not at that time I'd need to return to Ava.

"Ava," I said her name aloud, exhaling on it like a vow. The katra on my arms tingled. I'd given such a promise, like the way I uttered her name now, when I'd gotten my markings as every Rhonar warrior did at the age of maturity. Mine still glowed a faint red, the sign of my kedara—my life's energy—flowing through me.

Brok was of my *Brather*, and we each vowed, one to the other, along with twelve other warriors, who all chose to be as blood. Families were born, and while all warriors were brathers, the sacred vow to be "of my *Brather*" marked us as more than kin. We were soul-bound brathers. My markings showed that allegiance at the top of my shoulders, then it flowed to the symbols for my family on my biceps, and finally, to the sign for my empathic ability on my forearms. The space on my wrists was reserved for one thing, one hope only, and currently it was unmarked.

Would the katra flow and seal her name on my skin?

I allowed that thought, a brief fleeting sense of hope to fill my hearts. Although I didn't say it aloud yet, not to myself, not to Brok, and certainly not to the rest of my Rhonar brathers, I let it bubble up from the depths of my soul.

Truxoria. The miracle of the word filled my head in our ancient tongue, and then, just before the chamber door closed to cut me off from the feelings that churned inside me, I thought...*Mate.*

Chapter 7

AVA

"WHAT AN ASSHAT!" I PLOPPED ON THE BED, LEGS crisscrossed. "How dare he insinuate…" I shoved the sheet tighter around me. "I can't believe he even…"

I mumbled the bits and pieces of my scattered thoughts aloud, working myself into a good snit. It wasn't until the firelight began to dance from an errant draft that I finally allowed my mind to settle. "Okay, Ava. You're smarter than this." Rubbing my temples, I sucked in a breath and blew it free. Then, I did that three more times. "Let's put that education to some use this time, huh?"

Granted it hadn't helped me much while I was stuck in that cage, but surely I could decipher the psyche of a massive alien humanoid… "Did he say warrior?" And why was my brain focusing on that fact? Well, okay, I did recall him saying something about being a warrior, and he certainly looked the part. From his tight black pants and tall boots to his bare tattooed arms and leather-like armor across his chest. Plus, he was massive with a helluva body, like muscles-wise and size-wise. Not that I thought he was attractive or anything, right? *Right.* "Oh my god! This is not happening."

I was about two seconds away from a panic attack. I could feel the anxiety rising in my throat. *Breathe. In one, two. Out one, two.* I used my grounding technique like a lifeline. Attraction to a captor wasn't *that* out of the ordinary. They had a syndrome named after the concept for stars' sake. Viewing him from a detached outsider's perspective, it was clear he had physically appealing qualities. The eyes, for example. What person was going to see those royal blue eyes and think anything else? It was okay. I was fine.

Deep breath in.

Yes, he was very fit. Lots of muscles, and his chest was warm. *So, so warm.* I wrinkled my nose. Wait, why did I know that? I strained to grasp the memory. "The inside of a…carriage?" He had mentioned something like that, right? My mind filled in the blanks, showing me an old-fashioned carriage, like one from Earth's Victorian times. Warmth flowed down my neck and over my breasts as I recalled laying against something hot, and firm, and yet, so damn comfortable. I shivered, but not from the cold.

"And this isn't helping." I shook my head and laid on my stomach once more. What was the sense in thinking on it further? I wasn't getting anymore answers with my mind spinning in every direction, and since I couldn't trust my own stupid brain at the moment, I might as well try to relax. That was my conclusion anyway, until a soft knock at the door distracted me.

"Greetings, may I come in?" A soft feminine voice flowed from beyond the door.

I wasn't altogether certain I was ready for more company, but I found myself sitting up and saying, "Yes."

The woman that entered was like none I'd ever seen, an occurrence that was becoming all too common in my experience. She had soft lavender skin and large black anime eyes. Her nose was so small at the center of her long oval face. Pearly white hair ran to her hip in a single side braid thrown over her right shoulder. She appeared somehow both middle-aged and ageless at the same time.

"Hello, I'm Maena," she said, giving me a small nod as she carried a tray atop her outstretched hands. "I've brought you Verebog tea. It helps to heal the body and soothe the mind." Setting it on the side table beside the water goblet Xelan had given me earlier, she poured us each a cup.

"Thank you. I'm Ava," I said as I reached for the cup she offered and tried not to flinch. She was kind and soft-spoken, not at all threatening. But her double-knuckled fingers made my spine stiffen. Had I been back on the ship with my fellow human scientists and encountered her as our first alien contact, I wouldn't have given her hands a second thought. Yet here, now, after everything I'd been through, they rattled me.

She seemed to sense my unease and gave me an understanding smile. Pulling the chair to the side of the bed, she sat and sipped the tea. "You must have so many questions. I know I did when the Rhonar first saved my partner and me."

I sat up straighter at that. "Saved you?"

"Oh yes." She smiled wider and rested the teacup in her lap. "It was a harrowing experience." Her body vibrated for an instant, as if the memory caused physical discomfort. "My Tallis and I were on holiday and planning to travel to Sense VII. It's a popular vacation spot among my people." She set the tea aside and folded her fingers together. "Our cruiser sprung a fuel leak. We thought it had been fully repaired during our supply stop, but sadly, it seemed we'd been tagged by pirates."

"Pirates?" I sipped from my cup. The tea was perfectly flavorful and not too hot, just the way I preferred it. But I was too immersed in Maena's story to fully appreciate it. "What happened?"

"Well, on these space outposts, especially in the Meta Sector where Sense VII is located as well as Craxon, the planet you're on now, pirates are a problem for all law-abiding species. You see, the Meta Sector is a complicated part of the universe, where laws are regularly broken and corruption commonplace." She sighed, her hands visibly tightening in her lap.

"Unfortunately, it also houses the most prosperous and flourishing trade routes and viable planets in the known galaxies." Leaning closer, she lowered her voice as if revealing a secret. "Still, no one likes pirates. They tag ships that have booty they wish to steal and hunt down the owners in space. It's outlawed by all in the sector, even the gangs that fight over territory like children battling for a favored toy."

"Why doesn't anyone stop them?" I couldn't believe all that existed in the wide universe. Humanity was in for a rude awakening when they learned who and what we'd been sharing the stars with. That was, if I ever got home to tell them. Which made me wonder if pirates had attacked my ship, and what had happened to my companions aboard it. "What do they do after they hunt down a ship?"

"It depends on what they're after." Maena tugged at the strands of hair that fell loose at the end of her braid. "Sometimes they just take what they want and leave the owners and the ship floating in space. Other times, they take…" She freed her hair, undoing and then re-braiding it as if a nervous gesture. "Well, they take everything."

"Everything?" I recoiled. If I thought harder about it, I already suspected as much. I had only to examine where I ended up to know the truth. Yet hearing it aloud made the horror of it too real.

"Yes, everything and everyone. And they sell it all where they can." Maena fastened her hair and reached for the tea again. The cup shook in her hand. "It's terrible."

"I'm so sorry." Empathy for this alien washed through me. It seemed we had shared a similar experience, and I had no wish to cause her pain by asking her to relive it. "You don't have to tell me anymore. I think I can guess the rest."

"Oh no, I want to tell you. It's just that these pirates are so awful, and our journey after we were taken took quite some time before we arrived here. I won't talk about that part, if it's all right with you." Her oval eyes widened impossibly larger.

I nodded. "Of course, you can tell me whatever you're comfortable with."

"Thank you." She inhaled deeply from lips slightly darker than her lavender skin. "We were sold in the slave market like you were, but Xelan and Brokdar found us." She took another sip of her tea. "They offered us our freedom. They are honorable as are all the Rhonar warriors. But we couldn't accept. After we learned about their mission here, we wanted to remain and help them."

"Yes, Xelan did say something about that," I offered begrudgingly. My feelings about him were too conflicted to know the truth of his words, but with Maena, it was easier. I didn't spot any deception in her story, and her reactions seemed genuine. "He said they were undercover to stir rebellion from inside the ruling class."

"Exactly!" She clapped. "And now, the chance is getting closer. But, I'll let Xelan tell you more about that later. I've kept you up too long when you're just healing."

"Not at all. I'm glad you came to talk to me." I smiled, my first real smile in what felt like a long time.

"Well, I wanted you to know that you're safe. I know these warriors can seem…" She paused as if deciding on the right word.

"Dominant," I offered, although I instantly regretted the choice. It brought to mind too many suggestive images, and I could feel the blush rising to my cheeks.

"Yes, I suppose that's the word, isn't it?" Her laughter tinkled like a glass bell. "But they are truly good, if a bit intimidating. You'll see as you come to know them better." She rose from the chair, taking my now empty teacup and placing it on the tray beside hers. "Night is coming, and you'll need to stay warm. Brokdar will go with my Tallis tomorrow to procure you appropriate clothing. I'm afraid none of us wanted to leave while you were still unconscious. But now that you're awake and on the mend, we'll be sure you have everything you need."

"That's kind of you." I patted her arm in gratitude. "I'm thankful for all that you've done."

"Not at all, dear. I'm so happy we were able to get you out of that awful place." She shook her head, the heavy braid swinging behind her with the motion. "Now, I have a new medicine brewing that's going to make those wounds heal completely, but it takes time to prepare. So, you be patient, and do what Xelan says when he comes back."

I huffed and motioned to the bed. "What else do I need to do besides rest here?"

"Well, now. We're in the frost season and the temperature drops real low at night. We studied about Terrans while you were sleeping and learned your species can't handle this much cold. So let him help, yes?"

I refrained from rolling my eyes. "It doesn't feel that cold, and if I just have a heavier blanket, I'll be all right."

"Oh no. We can't risk putting anything too heavy on your back with your wounds as they are. For the rest of you it's fine, but not your back. I know you don't feel the pain with my herbal remedy, but until I can get this new medicine finished, we want to be careful." She waved toward the fireplace. "And we'll keep that burning, although you'll still need Xelan's help. He's gotten you through the last two nights while you slept. Just one more, and I promise by tomorrow, the medicine will be done and you'll be right as a Juvian bud in spring."

I giggled. I couldn't help it. Maena's optimism was infectious. "Okay. I don't know what a Juvian bud is, but I'll do as you say."

"That's a good patient." Her purple mouth quirked up. "I'm glad." Hoisting the tray onto her hip, she gave me a one-handed clap which made her fingers look like a duck's beak. I took it as a sign of goodbye and made the same motion back. "Rest well, Ava. I'll see you in the morning."

"Thank you again, Maena. Goodnight!" As the door shut quietly behind her, I realized I hadn't asked her the most important thing. *What exactly had she meant by letting Xelan help me?* I pondered the answer as I laid on the bed, staring into the pink flames. If the fire couldn't warm me, and a blanket on my back was out of the question, what could the alien warrior do?

Unbidden images sprang to mind. Xelan's warm muscled body spread over mine, pressing me into the mattress. His mouth on my neck, my breasts, kissing a path down my torso and hips, centering his focus on the apex of my thighs. A long, slow lick that would be all I'd need to set my temperature rising.

I moaned aloud, then clasped a hand over my traitorous mouth.

To be fair, it *would* keep me warm. I snorted at the thought. It had been a while since I'd made time for that kind of activity, preferring to focus on my career. And well, my last boyfriend hadn't quite been memorable in that department. An academic like me, he'd been nice and brilliant and…utterly disappointing in the bedroom. I mean no matter how hard I tried to spice it up from role play to dirty talk to toys, he wasn't into any of it. He was grade-A vanilla all the way. *Boring and predictable.*

I didn't mind vanilla every now and then. But I was more a rocky road gal, so I broke it off. Without much fanfare either, ending it the way it began with a conversation over coffee. It was all so very polite. And damn how I hated it.

"Hah! Look what I have now." I plopped my chin on my crossed arms. I had craved adventure, a chance to spread my wings and yeah, okay, explore my suppressed sexual side, if the chance arose. What I had not planned for was an abduction in space, a gray-skinned alien demon terrifying me, a creepy bug-man beating me, and a sexy alien warrior saving me. Because whether I trusted him or not, Xelan *had* saved me. I could admit that much. But anything after that? I just didn't know yet.

You'll have to decide soon. Fiddling with the blankets, I yanked one up to cover my lower half. The light was beginning to take on that dusk hue, when the world seemed to soften before nightfall. Even on another planet, I recognized the hour. It was my favorite time of day at home. Here, however, it signaled my reprieve from the captivating alpha alien's presence was almost at an end.

I tried to consider my options logically as I'd been taught, using the same scientific method I would with any other problem. Yet, the image of Xelan stretched out beside me, his chest gloriously bare, kept invading my thoughts.

"This is ridiculous," I grumbled aloud. "You're not some horny teenager." But no matter how I fought, the fantasy continued to grow as if my dry spell was kindling for the rising desire.

A madness came over me, and I found my hand slipping between the sheets. I glimpsed the setting sun outside, knowing I didn't have much time. "I'll be quick. I just need to take the damn edge off." I knew it was true. Despite the strangest of circumstances, I was so turned on that I'd never be able to think rationally when Xelan returned without some relief.

I closed my eyes and let my fingers wander, hoping that whatever had gripped me would let go before the big sexy alien returned. If it didn't, I wasn't sure what I'd do.

I groaned into the pillow, picturing a pair of royal blue eyes.

Chapter 8

XELAN

THE ISOLATION CHAMBER BEEPED THREE TIMES, ALERTING me to the end of its cycle. The door opened and I emerged as if born anew. At least, that's how I was supposed to feel after a round in the pod. It was my usual reset for balancing my empathic shields to a state of equilibrium. Instead a wave of lust so strong and intense nearly knocked me on my ass.

"What the crex?" My cock hardened with a demanding ache. I wore nothing under my leathers, since they were constructed to keep a male well protected during battle. I was glad for the mercy from additional fabric, but regretted my choice of the fighting gear as the strong material constrained my shaft painfully.

If I had any doubt before about Ava being my mate, I didn't any longer. Emotions, after suffering so long in the void, were a sure sign, but the true confirmation was this —the mating lust. Mated male pairings dedicated songs to it. The elders of our brathers who were mated before the tragedy struck, and our females were lost to the enemy's devastating weapon, told of it in stories. But I'd never thought to experience the state for myself. It was all consuming, even though two floors separated me from her. As if she were the light in an endless darkness, her presence called to me.

I bound up the stairs, three at a time. When I ran into Brok on the ground floor, I waved him off. Maena called to me next, but I barely got out a response. "Later," I said in a clipped tone. I knew I appeared out of my senses, and perhaps, I was. But nothing and no one would come between me and my goal—Ava.

On the second floor, I lightened my steps. I didn't want her to know of my approach. The little Terran had no idea of a Rhonar mate bond. From the research we could gather on her home world, a planet called Earth, her people had no such ties. They formed partnerships through trial and error, until they found someone—or sometimes multiple someones—to tie their life to. Others preferred to walk through life alone. None of it was the biological need that affected my kind. Would she even feel the beginnings of the bond?

"Crex." I hadn't considered that she might feel differently, or not feel it at all. When the mating lust began it was usually but a matter of time before the bond was sealed through consummation. How would I possibly explain? What if she didn't believe me? I yanked at my hair, willing inspiration to strike. "Can she deny the bond?" I had no idea what would happen to me if she did. I knew of no precedent for such a situation. My kind had only ever bonded with other Rhonar. I didn't even know if it was possible to bond with another species. Unless…

"It couldn't be." The idea was so ludicrous, it was almost laughable. "More mad than a Terran mate?" I spoke my thoughts aloud, working through the idea that gripped me, even as the mating lust continued to hammer at me. "Earth…Terrans…could it be a lost colony?" It would explain why I was able to feel the bond with one, despite none of my kind experiencing the mating lust with another species before. If these Terrans were Rhonar descendants, the very ones my brathers even now searched for, the connection would be in their kedara. The life blood that flowed through their veins would be a direct link to us. I'd think on it more and talk it over with Brok, but later, much later, after the mating lust was sated.

I strode with new purpose toward her door. With my palm wrapped around the handle, I took a deep breath, going over everything I'd say to convince her of the truth I knew in my bones. She was *mine*.

As I entered her room on silent feet, I was hit with an erotic sight that fired my blood hotter than I believed possible. In the center of the bed my little Truxoria had hitched up one leg toward her chest. She remained on her stomach, her back protected from the heavy blanket that tangled around her outstretched leg. With a low cry, she worked her fingers between the apex of her thighs.

All of my focus narrowed to that spot. If I'd been threatened by blindness for my staring, I still could not have looked away.

Her moans turned frantic. Then, a small distressed sound and her pained frustration hit me, shaking me from my fascination with the sensual act. "Ava," I tried gently, knowing she'd be disturbed by my presence.

"Ah," she squealed and rolled over in her surprise, falling off the bed.

I grabbed her before she could land on the cold floor and pulled her tight to my chest. "You're all right."

"No, I am not all right." She half-sobbed the words, and the sorrow radiating from her tore holes in each of my hearts. "I don't know what's wrong with me."

Climbing on the bed, I leaned back against the stone headboard and cradled her in my arms. I hummed and uttered nonsense in her ear while she clutched my biceps and buried her head in my neck. Her tears flowed freely as if all the pain she'd endured could no longer be contained.

After several minutes, her sobs turned to soft sniffs. She exuded such loss as she looked up at me, droplets clinging to her lovely lashes. My instincts pushed at me to raise my empathic shields against her emotions, but I couldn't. I wanted to, needed to feel everything from her, even the bad.

"I'm sorry." She stiffened suddenly in my arms, then pulled away. "I don't know what came over me."

"I do." I gave her the blanket to hold in front of her breasts. The last thing I wanted to do was cover her. Yet in her sadness, the lust had temporarily abated for both of us, as if knowing my beautiful mate needed something else first. I wiped a stray tear from her cheek. "You have nothing to be ashamed of," I added as the rosy hue returned to her skin. "You have been strong, and it would be strange if you didn't set free your grief."

"No, that makes sense." She swiped at her nose. "I'm not embarrassed about crying, although I am sorry I cried all over you."

I shrugged. "I'm not. I'm glad you trust me with such things."

She didn't deny that, which I took as a positive sign. Yet her hands twisted the blanket in her grip. "It's just that..." Loosening one hand, she shifted to tugging her hair. "I'd never in front of..." The pink flush rose higher, covering her neck and cheeks. "I didn't mean for you to..."

Oh, it was shyness then. I grinned inwardly, unable to resist the urge to tease my mate. "You didn't wish for me to see you touching yourself?"

She yelped. "Of course not! I'm not some exhibitionist."

"But you're so perfect." I breathed in, catching the scent of her lingering arousal. "How could I resist watching?"

"Whoa." She held up her hand palm out. "Hold on there, buddy. You walked in on me. And besides, I don't normally act that way. Something came over me."

I nodded solemnly. "Yes, and it's affected me as well."

"You?" As she shifted from sitting to kneeling on the bed, she brought her legs tightly together. It did nothing to hide her enticing scent. "Why am I feeling so…" She waved toward her lower half. "You know."

"Aroused?" I offered.

She sucked in a breath, desire stirring once more. "Yes."

"It is what my people call the mating lust." I scanned her face for her reaction.

Her pert nose twitched. "And what exactly is that?"

Drav it all. I knew I'd have to explain. I tried to grasp what I'd come up with earlier. "It's what happens when a Rhonar male finds his Truxoria."

"Trux-what now?" She leaned on her right side as if to get more comfortable.

I yearned to tug her into my arms again. With her bout of grief having passed, at least for now, my desire was steadily rising too. "Truxoria. It's the sacred word for mate in the ancient tongue."

"And what does this have to do with us?"

I raised a brow at her. My mate was smart. Although I knew so little about her, I wanted to learn everything.

But her intelligence? I'd already gleaned that. And she understood what was implied.

She gasped. "No, that's," she bolted upright, a palm over her mouth, "that's impossible."

"I thought so too, at first. It's why I needed to leave before." I cocked my knee and wrapped my arms around it, more so to prevent me from reaching for her again than comfort. "You see, Rhonar males lose their emotions when they reach maturity and experience two states after—the hunger and the void."

Her eyes widened, the light from the fire dancing in them. "That doesn't sound pleasant."

"It's not. It's a difficult existence," I admitted through a clenched jaw. Now that I had found my mate it was challenging to think of never experiencing her warmth. She had saved me from a cold, empty existence, even if she didn't yet know it. "The only way to regain emotions is to find one's mate. It's what happened to me."

Although she crossed her arms over her chest with the sheet firmly tucked underneath, she seemed to be considering my words. "When you collapsed, that's when it hit you, right?"

"Yes." I was stunned by her perceptive mind. "Our mated warriors say it's different for each Rhonar male, but I'd begun to feel the stirrings of emotions upon first seeing you. I just didn't recognize them as mine."

She tilted her head as if in question. "Why not?"

In truth, it was becoming more of an effort to speak. The lust returned now in full force, and I could scent the answering arousal from her. Yet I had to tell her. "I have an empathic ability. I can sense emotions in others, and so, I didn't realize that what I was feeling was stemming from me."

"Oh!" she cried. "That's fascinating." Her eyes zipped back and forth like she were solving a great puzzle in her head.

"Well, I suppose. But it kept growing, and then, when you told me your name—"

"You recognized the emotions," she interrupted, excitement apparent in her tone.

"Not quite. It was more like I'd been hit by a meteor. Everything compounded at once into a giant spiraling ball." My spine stiffened at the memory. While I wouldn't trade the discovery of my mate for anything, it hadn't exactly been pleasurable to be bombarded with all those emotions.

"And that's when you collapsed." She lowered herself onto her side again and plopped a fist under her chin. "Makes sense."

"Yes, and after that initial recognition, " I said carefully as we were arriving at the pinnacle of our current predicament, "the mating lust began."

"This is so interesting. I'd love to write a paper about it." Her eyes flashed as if she were already forming a report in her head, but her expression changed. Her legs grew restless beneath the blanket, and a soft moan passed her lips. "Oh stars, what am I talking about?" She sat up a third time. "You're not speaking theory here. You're talking about us, aren't you?"

I moved slowly, achingly slowly toward her. Like prey caught in a trap, her breathing grew rapidly. "Yes, Ava," I said soft and steady. "We are mates."

"But..." Her lower lip trembled. The uncertainty wafting off her hit me in the gut. "Wh-what does that mean? Like in your culture?"

"It means," I reached for her, wrapping my fingers around her shoulder gently, "if you'll let me, I'd like to help you through this mating lust."

"How?" Her gaze narrowed, the distrust darkening her features.

"I'd never do anything you didn't wish me to." As I said the words, I knew them to be true. I'd always put her first, her health and happiness above all. I chose not to tell her everything about the mate bond yet, but not out of deception. I simply didn't know how to explain that a Rhonar, once mated, had no other. For me, Ava was my Truxoria, my mate, my world. Nothing and no one would ever mean more. Yet, would it be the same for her? She felt the lust, but would she be bound to me as I to her after mating sex solidified our bond? I didn't know, but I'd have to tell her. I'd give her the choice to complete our bond or not.

But…not yet.

For now, I had to ease this rising lust between us. Then, I'd convince her to be mine, truly mine, forever. Somehow.

"I believe you." She chewed on her lip and her hand came up to grab my forearm. "Please. I can't take this."

I breathed in her scent, letting it fill my lungs. "We need to satiate the desire."

"I'm not," she tightened her grip, even as she fought to stifle a moan, "n-not sleeping with you."

It took my translator a beat to determine that Ava didn't mean simply sleeping. "I understand. And I promise you, we won't cross that boundary." I guided her onto her side, careful not to further injure her tender back. "Trust me, my Truxoria. You're safe with me."

As the hunger within her grew, swirling through me and adding to my own, I stretched out beside her. For the last two nights, I had done so while she slept to keep her warm. Now, I did so for an entirely different reason, and the pleasure of having her awake and eager for my touch was almost too much to endure. My emotional shields held no protection from her, and as intense as it was, I wanted none. To share so intimately with my mate, the sole being in the universe destined as my match, was like nothing else. I longed to unite with her, to bond her to me for all time.

She sighed as I let my fingers trail along the sheet, inching it down her body with each pass.

That was not to be, not yet. I had to convince her of our connection, to show her how amazing it could be between us. I had no problem complying with that need. I caressed her arm from shoulder to elbow, then back up again. Her skin was soft and lush. Leaning over her, I kissed along her neck with a feather light touch. Nuzzling at her ear, I growled, "Will you let me taste you?"

Her sharp intake of breath gave me my answer. In time her heart would come around to what her body already knew. Oh yes, she was mine. And tonight, I'd show her.

Chapter 9

AVA

THIS WAS INSANE. I'D GONE INSANE. IT WAS THE ONLY explanation as to why I was letting this alien have his way with my body. Even now, he was peppering my neck with gentle kisses that drove me wild. I grabbed his hair and moaned his name, "Xelan."

"Drav it, Ava. You have no idea what that does to me." He groaned and redoubled his efforts.

Oh I had an idea. The same thing his touch was doing to me. I'd never been so turned on in my life. The evidence of my arousal spread to my thighs. I didn't care. I wanted more. Earlier, when the lust had hit me like a tsunami, I'd pictured him beside me, touching me, tasting me. But the reality was better, so much better than I'd imagined it. And we'd barely begun.

I noticed absently that the temperature had dropped, but Xelan radiated heat like a furnace. I burrowed into that warmth, stretching my limbs so I was wrapped up in him. The markings on his arms glowed softly. Then, he put his mouth to mine, delving inside and showing me all the things he could do with that tongue. Stars, it was everything. I felt hot and on edge, like I'd come out of my skin if he didn't take me soon.

"Xelan," I whimpered against his mouth.

"I know, mate. I know." He didn't waste time in teasing me further. His hand sought my pussy, and I opened for him greedily. My top leg draped over his waist. He still wore his leathers, and I noted absently how uncomfortable that must be. But before I could tell him it was okay to remove them, his knuckle brushed my clit.

"More," I cried, frantic in my desire. I ground my hips against his hand.

He circled my clit with firm strokes. "Come for me, Truxoria." His voice was deep and growly in my ear. Every nerve fired like a bow strung too tight. I wanted to fall, to let myself go. I needed to. Something held me back. "Give in. Let go." He plunged two long, thick fingers inside me. His thumb pressed against my clit. "NOW."

"Oh fuck. Yes!" I gripped his shoulders. Hard. My body bucked as he rode out the waves of my orgasm. My pussy clenched against his invading fingers. Idly, I wished it was his cock. That thought broke through some of the lust-filled haze and afterglow to bring a fresh wave of reality.

I was in bed with an alien who thought I was his mate.

My eyes popped open, and I peered into his half-lidded gaze. Blue, the gorgeous depths of blue, stared back at me. Yet, even as I fought to hold on to rational thoughts, I couldn't summon up any real ire over the situation. Yes, this was not ideal. I was abducted and held as a slave on a backwards planet. But all things considered, I wasn't in bad shape. Hell, my master—and like it or not, that's what he was at present—was a sexy-as-sin Rhonar warrior. I might not have any idea about his species, but he was humanoid, and well…it just felt…right.

Okay, I was definitely crazy.

"You…" I wasn't sure what to say after our encounter, but as my leg was still hung over his waist, I felt the brush of the top of his pants on my calf. "Why don't you put on something more comfortable? Those pants can't be good to sleep in."

He smiled, and the expression changed his face from sexy to downright lethal. "You're right. But usually, I don't sleep in anything."

I shot him a half-grin. I couldn't help it. His teasing tone was light, even a little boyish. It was so different from the dominant male who demanded my orgasm mere moments ago. I liked both sides. "That may be crossing our boundary line."

"Of course. Wouldn't want that." He chuckled and rose from the bed. Instantly, the temperature dropped, and I reached for the blanket. He put a restraining hand on my arm. "Not over your back. And don't worry, I'm just going to the dresser here. I'll be right back to keep you warm." His smirk told another tale. "Besides, that was only the beginning. I'm not done with you yet. Not by far."

Oh hell. I had no idea what I was in for, but my body had no problem with it. Even now, what couldn't be more than a minute or two after my orgasm, the lust rose again. My breasts felt heavy, the tender buds stiffening in the chilled air. I rubbed my thighs together to quench the unbearable ache, but my pussy throbbed like a second heartbeat. Whether I wanted to believe Xelan or not, it was clear that I'd been affected by the mating lust. No other explanation could account for this maddening level of arousal.

I felt hornier than a damned teenager. How could I deny him in this state?

"I can't," I mumbled under my breath. If I were honest with myself, I didn't want to. It wasn't just my out-of-control libido talking either. I might not have known him well, but I was drawn to the dark-haired alien. His strange, shifting tattoos that glowed faintly in the firelight, his demanding yet gentle demeanor, his otherworldly blue eyes, and yeah, his rock hard muscles all culminated into a package that I was unable to resist.

You have to resist. A little voice whispered in my mind as Xelan approached the bed. He sported a pair of soft sleep pants that did nothing to hide the massive erection beneath. I pushed the nagging voice aside. Maybe I'd gone mad, but I was not about to turn this male away. Consequences be damned.

"Are you ready for me, Ava?" His words sent a shiver along my spine. I looked up, and up, and up. When he stood over me, I felt small and delicate, but still…safe. Somehow he radiated both danger—the sexy kind I wanted to dive into—and safety. It was the best combination, one that lit my already burning desire into an inferno.

"Yes," I said. Rising to my knees put me eye-level with his chest. I grabbed on to his trim waist and ran my tongue along one flat copper nipple.

He groaned. "Enough of that, my mate."

I pouted my lips as he guided me to lie on my side, a hand tangling in my hair. "Why?"

"I have other plans." He fluffed a pillow under my head, then moved beside me. His lips found my neck again, kissing and sucking the tender flesh. When I was squirming under his ministrations, he kissed a path lower. His tongue teased along the slopes of my breasts and circled my peaks without ever touching them. My legs moved restlessly and my hands gripped his dark locks.

"Xelan, please," I begged. The fire rose in me, fast and wild.

"Patience, little one." He smiled against my breast. "So needy."

"I'm not that little." I snorted. "Or *that* needy."

He flicked his tongue against my right nipple, and he had to hold my hips to keep me from coming off the bed. "Oh no?" he said. Then he licked again, and again, as I cried and pleaded and tugged his hair. When he fixed his lips around the swollen bud and sucked, I swore I saw stars.

"It's too much."

His answer was to do it all over again to my left breast. "It's not enough," he said in that deep voice. "Not yet." As he at last turned his attentions from my breasts, he pushed onto his forearms and gave me that half-lidded stare. "Roll onto your stomach."

"What?" I gasped. I couldn't imagine what he was thinking.

"Do it, Ava." He moved to the end of the bed by my knees. "Don't make me tell you again."

The urge to argue bubbled below the surface. When had I, an independent, professional woman, and a scientist for stars' sake, taken orders in bed? *Never.* With my vanilla ex, and the guy before that, and well, that one fling in college, I'd always been the dominant partner. I knew what I wanted, it was just getting someone to give it to me. At least, that's what I'd thought. I hadn't imagined I'd enjoy being on the submissive end. Yet, if the drenched sheet twisted around my thighs was any indication, I liked it…a lot.

"Yes, Master," I said sarcastically, turning onto my stomach. If he wanted me to play the role of slave, then I'd at least get some enjoyment from it in bed.

He swatted my ass. It wasn't hard, but it was a clear warning.

I yelped.

"Behave, Truxoria." He rubbed the spot where he'd smacked. "Now, lift your hips."

Glancing at him over my shoulder, I asked, "Why?"

He responded by arching a brow at me.

"Fine." I huffed. With my bottom in the air and the sheet slipping to my knees, I was utterly exposed. I fisted the pillow under my head, dragging it to support my chest and chin. The firelight danced tantalizingly in the hearth and cast long shadows on the walls. I shivered at the loss of his body heat beside me. "Is this what you want?"

"Almost." Slipping lower on the bed, he grabbed my knee and split me wider. I couldn't see exactly what he was doing from this angle, but suddenly, his nose was rubbing the inside of my thigh.

"What are you—?

He slapped my ass again. "Shh. No more questions. Just feel."

As if I could do anything else.

Xelan shifted, lying on his back, and slipped his head under my hips. "That's right, mate. It's time to taste you."

Oh fuck. That's what he'd meant. His tongue ran along the spot where my thigh met my pelvis. I nearly collapsed. "I don't know if I can stay upright." He hadn't come close to my pussy and I was already melting.

"Then, come down. Come down and let me lick your sweet honey." He growled, and the sound vibrated through me. "Let me have what's mine."

I had no control. None at all. And I didn't want any.

He wrapped his arms around my thighs splitting me wider and bringing my aching pussy to his lips. The first lick was hot and wet and…perfect.

"Ohhhh." Any chill I felt by him not being at my side was negated by the flames singeing along my nerves. He played my body like an instrument. I came alive under his expert caresses.

He licked from the bottom of my slit to the top of my pussy, taking extra care to circle and flick my clit. At first, it was slow, rhythmic movements that mirrored his actions on my breasts. Then, as if sensing my desire, the speed and pressure increased. It increased like a…wait…

"Oh my god." His tongue was vibrating. It was actually fucking vibrating. "Xelan?"

He didn't respond, but the vibrations from that magical tongue sent my orgasm spiraling. As the waves crashed through me, Xelan latched onto my clit and thrust his fingers inside me. My pussy clamped down, throbbing and pulsing. He stayed with me, pumping his fingers and gently sucking at my clit. The pleasure continued as if one orgasm led into the other.

I'd never been able to reach the peak more than once in the same night. Hell, it was usually hard to get there at all, at least with a partner. And now, I'd lost track of how many times I'd come. If it kept going, was that one, or did the ebbs and flows count as more?

I might have been delirious.

With infinite care, Xelan brought me back from the incredible high. He licked along my nether lips, cleaning up every last drop as if he couldn't get enough. When he'd kissed my thighs and pussy clean, he slid out from under me. He helped lower my hips, and turned me to lie on my side. It was then I noticed the bulge in his pants.

"Wait," I said, a hand clasped on his leg as he rose. "What about you?"

He smiled down at me. "I'm quite satisfied, little one."

"But, you didn't," I released him to wave in the direction of his cock, "you know."

Kneeling, he was still too tall for me to be at eye level but he met my gaze with a bow of his head. "It wasn't about that, my Truxoria. I wanted, needed to feel you on my tongue." His stare intensified as if searching for my soul. "It's a desire that hits all Rhonar males, to know, to taste." He angled his mouth to mine, sharing my special flavor with me. "And I'll always crave you."

"That's…" I didn't know what to say. I'd never been with a selfless lover before. And certainly not with anyone who looked at me like I was the center of their universe. "Nice?"

He laughed. "It is. If you would, however, grant me one request?"

Oh, so there *was* a catch. Wasn't there always? My heart sank. "What is it?"

"I'd like to hold you while we rest." He ran a hand over his chin as if he was contemplating a problem. "I wasn't sure how to tell you, but the truth is, I've had to lie beside you while you were unconscious. As you've felt, the weather here grows frigid at night, and we couldn't keep you warm enough without my body heat."

He wanted to…cuddle? Okay, he couldn't be real. No way in hell did this hot alien warrior want to cuddle after licking me into the stratosphere and not even getting off himself. *And what about the other part?* The insidious little voice that sounded a lot like my mother returned. But how was I supposed to be upset about that? Yeah, it was a bit creepy that he'd been lying next to me while I was so vulnerable, but his explanation was reasonable. I could feel the cold even now as he stood beside me. I wouldn't have made it through the night without his help. And well, he'd given me the best orgasms of my life without asking for a thing in return, except to cuddle. How was a girl supposed to be mad about that?

"Yes," I said without hesitation. I opened my arms to him, making it clear that I wanted him to hold me.

The smile that spread across his face was a sight to behold. It made him beautiful in a completely masculine and devastating way.

"You honor me." He slid underneath the sheet, careful to avoid my injured back, and brought me against his hard chest.

I was so warm and content, more so than I'd ever been in my life as I burrowed into his side. So, it was to my surprise when that nagging voice popped up again. *Don't you want to go home?* It demanded. *Don't you want to be free? You're a slave here. His slave.*

I bit my lip, wondering about it. If we could continue to play out this fantasy in the bedroom, I'd have fun exploring this side of me. But that was role-play for pleasure. What about the reality of my situation? To be seen as less than, to be someone's property? That wasn't me. I might like Xelan, and stars knew he was the most amazing lover I'd ever had, but give up my life, my independence, my freedom for him?

No. I'd never.

His quiet breaths turned slowly deeper. I snuck a peek at his face through my lashes, my cheek resting against his chest. His brow was softer in sleep, the worry lines evening. I could not imagine what his life had been. To feel the emotions of those around me without ever getting to experience any of my own? That would have been its own kind of torment.

I sighed. My heart was softening toward this alien warrior. The tremors of deeper emotions plagued me, but no amount of desire could change our reality. And it left me uneasy as I drifted off to sleep, the last thought echoing across my mind.

Had I made a huge mistake?

Chapter 10

XELAN

As the early morning light cast the room in an orange hue, I stared at the little female asleep on my chest. Flecks of sunbeams shone on her thick black hair. Her skin was so soft, far different from my own, and her cheeks were rosy from the warmth she claimed from me. If I could, I'd give her every last speck of heat. I wanted her to always remain connected to me, especially now as my kedara urged me to claim her. My life's blood flowed hot as the need to bond her to me intensified.

I ignored it.

To hold her in my arms was the greatest gift. She had given me back emotions, forever altering the course of my life. I would not rush her into anything and focus instead on the gratitude I felt for my Truxoria. Even if my cock rose achingly beneath the sheet and flames of desire engulfed me. As a warrior, I'd long ago mastered control over my body, and it would not dictate my actions now.

I inhaled deeply, pulling her scent into my lungs.

Ava had changed everything. If I bonded with this small Terran, then it meant others of my kind could as well. The Rhonar would no longer face extinction. It was a humbling thought. Although Earth did not yet know of our existence, we had to find the planet and negotiate a treaty. It meant that our deadline to aid the rebellion had gone up.

We need to find evidence. Ever since arriving on Craxon and posing as members of the ruling class, we'd been trying to uncover the network of power holders. If we could prove the existence of this web of masterminds who controlled the economic and political movements, we'd be able to convince the holdouts and gain enough support for the rebellion to ignite. They just needed proof, and then, they'd have the numbers.

Now, more than ever, I wanted to be done with this mission and get off this drav planet.

As if in answer to my thoughts, a knock came at the door. "My sir and lady, are you well?"

I laughed aloud, causing Ava to stir. I couldn't resist. Joy, real joy washed over me so easily, and I reveled in it. "Come in, Maena, and stop being so formal."

Ava yelped, sitting upright and jerking the sheet to her. "Get off, she'll see us." She pushed at my hip, which made me laugh harder.

"Maena knows I've been sleeping beside you. She's the one who figured out it would keep you warm in the first place."

The door began to open. "She doesn't know everything," Ava hissed. "And she might know some, but she doesn't need to *see* it."

My laugher grew belly deep as Maena entered. She took in the sight and smiled. "What's all this?"

I rolled from the bed, rising and turning toward our guest with a grin plastered on my face. "My mate is afraid for you to see us together."

"Your," the expression of awe on her lavender face filled my joy to overflowing, "mate?"

"That's right." I waited as the words sank in. Maena's happiness matched my own. She squealed, a high-pitched note that carried throughout the house. Brok and Tallis came running at the noise, their steps heavy and urgent.

"What's wrong?" Brok entered first, his impressive frame taking up most of the space in the room.

Tallis followed after, finding a spot next to his wife as the room grew crowded. "What is it, my love?"

Ava appeared ready to bolt, so I sat back down and took her hand in mine. "Celestia has been kind." I kissed her knuckles, holding her gaze a moment before I turned to Brok. "I have found my Truxoria."

For as long as I had known Brok, he had always been stoic and serious. Even before we'd risen to malehood and begun the biological cycles of our kind, he rarely displayed emotion. Although he still suffered in the void, the shock that gripped him wafted like a cloud beyond my empathic shield. The surprise of finding a mate was too much for the void to block.

"Is it true?" His hands fisted at his sides as if he were fighting an inner battle.

I rose again so I could look him in the eye as I said, "It's true, my friend." I placed a reassuring hand on his shoulder. "It's real."

His expression shifted to a neutral countenance. "That's a gift from the universe." He bowed his head. "We must inform our brathers and give thanks to Celestia."

"We will, but first, we need to finish our mission here."

"Oh," Maena chimed in. Her lavender arm was looped through her husband's purple one, but she untangled their limbs to reach inside a pocket at the front of her flowing dress. "This came in just a little while ago." She handed me an envelope. Then, procuring a small tin from deeper in her pocket, she added, "And I brought this for Ava."

"Thank you," my mate said automatically. I could feel the confusion wafting off her at the conversations taking place, but she was polite nonetheless.

"Is that the medicine?" I asked Maena, holding the envelope aside and pointing at the tin.

"Yes. It took longer than I'd like, but it'll heal her right up now. Indeed, it will."

Tallis gave his wife a look that shone with pride, and it radiated from him in waves that felt like a burst of sunshine to my psyche. "You did so well."

Now that I had a mate to ground me and free my emotions, the feelings from others I had once despised no longer seemed a burden. In truth, I marveled at the sensations surrounding me from Maena's happiness at her creation to Tallis' delight in his wife's accomplishment to even Ava's curiosity. If only Brok could be saved from the void, my satisfaction would be complete.

"I'll be okay now?" Ava asked, her uncertainty apparent.

"Yes, my dear." Maena plopped on a corner of the bed, holding out the tin. "If you'll allow me to help you, this will heal you up in no time."

A pang of jealousy hit me unexpectedly in the gut. "I'll take care of it."

"I'm afraid not," Maena said patiently. "No dallying with your lady. You have business to take care of."

Before I could argue, Tallis cut in, "She's right, you know." He waved at the envelope I held in my fist. "That needs attending to."

Flipping it over, I eyed the paper. The large cursive script and crimson seal of the Craxion Elite, Lord Denthar Calth, met my gaze. I ground my back teeth together. If the item I held was what I thought, we'd be closer to our goal, but goddess, how I longed to make that crexing bastard pay. "The invitation?"

"Looks like it." Brok leaned against the wall, arms folded across his wide chest.

"Then we need a plan." I grabbed my clothes from where I had left them at the foot of the bed. "All right, Brok, Tallis, meet me in the study in five minutes. Maena, if you would attend Ava?"

"Of course." She shot me a look that was full of maternal-like indulgence. "Now, run along, and perhaps catch a shower and a change of clothes before your plotting session?"

The rising amusement that rolled through me made me feel years younger. I glanced down at my sleep pants and the worn clothes draped over my arm. "Good idea." I called to Brok and Tallis who had wisely headed for the hall. "Make that ten minutes."

"Good idea indeed." She laughed and rose from the bed. "Now, Ava dear, I'll put this on you when this silly male leaves, and then I'll fetch you some clothes and a nice breakfast. Once that medicine does its job, you won't have to worry about keeping your back uncovered."

Knowing my mate was in good hands did nothing to quell my nerves. Leaving her, even for a short while, was difficult. I strode toward her, and bending so our faces were level, I gave her a quick kiss on her cheek. I wanted more, much more, but I didn't dare as the mating lust was still strong in us both. Until it was fully sated, it would be an ever-present ache.

I welcomed it.

"I'll see you soon," I whispered to her. And with that, I turned and headed out. If I glanced behind me, I'd never leave the room.

It was harder than I'd imagined to shower alone and tug on a new pair of leathers and my chest armor after. Ava was only across the hall but the pain of even that short distance ate at me. It was an insatiable pull like an arrow drawn to a target. I longed to return to her; instead, I crossed the hall and descended the stairs to the study below where Brok and Tallis waited.

Together, we would come up with a plan. We had been angling for an invitation to one of the Craxion Elite's notorious parties. It was at this event we'd be able to gather the evidence we needed to incite the rebellion. We just needed to figure out how.

Steeling my heart against returning to Ava, I brought up my empathic shield. It was strange to be so cut off from the emotions of others now that I had embraced my own, but I would need all of my wits to focus on the task. I took a long, slow breath and prepared for the challenge ahead.

🪐

AVA

The medicine had worked as well as Maena promised. After she'd helped apply it to my back, she'd shown me how to adjust the shower and said I'd be clear to use it in two spans. I took that to mean hours and estimated the time by the light in the room.

The shower had not been quite what I was expecting. The stall itself didn't appear too out of the ordinary, except for the black tiles on all sides, base, and top. It was kind of like stepping into a sound booth instead of a shower. I pressed the buttons she'd shown me, and a goopy glittery gel, like the texture of pudding, came out of the overhead spigot. It had slid across my body as disgusting as slime. But before I had a chance to wipe it off, a blast of foam with the consistency of whip cream hit me. It cleaned all the gel away and then dissolved until nothing was left. I didn't even need a towel.

I had stepped from the shower stall and stared at the diamond-shaped *reflector* as Maena had called it. After a thin ray of light scanned my body, the reflector projected a three-dimensional image of me. It was a bit disorienting to see a smaller version of myself spinning in slow motion in front of me, but it did work better than a mirror. Staring at the image, I was shocked to find that the wounds on my back were not only healed, but completely gone. Not a single scar.

"I have to thank her again." I'd vowed to do so as I continued to analyze my projection.

It was fascinating technology. Once the device had my scan, it altered the projected image as I made adjustments. Like when I combed my fingers through my hair—which was surprisingly clean and smooth—it showed the changes on the projection.

"Amazing." I'd pulled my hair into a low ponytail with the hair ties Maena had left me. "She really thought of everything." I'd smiled as I peered into her basket of care items.

I hadn't taken too long in the bathroom, preferring to put on clean clothes for the first time in days. The clothes she'd left strewn on the dresser were soft and delicate looking, as if they were made for some fantasy fae creature. Except for my height, I didn't think I'd qualify. I'd gotten my mother's short stature, a gift passed along to the women in our family for generations, dating all the way back to the Edo period in Japan. But my hips were too wide, thanks to my father's Mediterranean ancestors, to ever be considered petite. Nevertheless, I was all for body positivity, and so I'd slipped on a whisper thin, dusty rose dress. It flared at the waist and fell to my knees. The top was a halter style that crossed over my breasts and tied at the neck.

"Talk about feminine." I'd twirled, making the skirt puff. Although I usually opted for practical slacks and blouses for work, and yoga pants and over-sized t-shirts at home, I had to admit, the dress made me feel good.

The day went by slowly but Maena visited again. We talked over lunch before she returned to whatever duties she needed to attend. When she left, I tugged the strange black chair over to the window and contented myself with watching the world outside. It was a strange one, and a planet, according to Maena, that desperately needed changing. That was what she, Xelan, and the others were fighting for—true change. Since I'd been sold here as a slave, I could get on board with that idea.

I tried not to think too much about the alien warrior who'd shared my bed, but no matter how hard I focused my thoughts away from him, they kept straying back. I knew two things to be true. First, I wanted to help on the mission. If Xelan and I had any real chance, then I couldn't remain a slave. Even if this were only a temporary assignment for him, I needed an end goal, and if that was inciting a rebellion on this planet, well, I'd yet to run from a fight. And stars knew I'd had my share of battles in the academic arena. Maybe it wasn't quite the same as an uprising, but I wasn't going to run from the challenge.

The second, and infinitely more complex, thought was that I wanted the blue-eyed alien. Whether it was this all-consuming mate lust or...deeper feelings, I didn't know yet. But I had my suspicions, and if he were everything he seemed to be, everything Maena assured me that he was, I wanted to give him a chance. Alien or not, he was the best man I'd met in a long time, and it wasn't just my libido talking. Although his masterful bedroom expertise—and yeah, okay, the vibrating tongue—didn't hurt his chances.

And so, I was staring out the window, not seeing anything really, as I contemplated these swirling feelings, when Xelan returned. The planet's sun—or possibly suns, it was hard to say—had dipped lower on the horizon, shining the orange light through the white curtains. I smiled at him.

"I know you believe we're mates," I said, rising to meet him. "And I'm willing to give us a chance, on one condition?"

His answer was immediate. "Anything."

"I was hoping you'd say that." I took his larger hand in mine, holding it tight so he'd know I was serious. "Maena told me what you're doing on this planet. How you've been waiting on this invitation to gather evidence for the holdouts of the rebellion." Nervous butterflies took flight in my stomach. I'd never shied away from stating my desires before, and I always went after what I wanted. But this was different somehow. I took a breath. "What I want…" I squeezed his palm. "What I need…" I brought it to rest between my breasts. "Is to be a part of the mission."

His eyes grew wide, and he opened his mouth to speak, but I laid my free hand over his lips.

"I am coming with you to that party."

Chapter 11

AVA

It took an incredible amount of convincing to get Xelan to accept, but surprisingly Brokdar—or Brok as he insisted I call him—agreed with me.

"It will be far more likely for an Elite to attend the party with a female slave." He'd turned to me and bowed his head. "Not that you'll be one for long."

"Thank you, Brok." I'd shot him a smile as Xelan had paced the hallway.

After I'd stated the reasons for me to come on the mission, he'd growled and escaped the room. I hadn't been deterred, simply following behind and calmly continuing my arguments. I was no stranger to stating my case. Dogged persistence is how I'd risen so high in the academic arena. Brok had found us like that, and upon hearing my side of it, he concurred.

Xelan looked like a child whose favorite toy had been snatched away, and it took everything in me not to laugh. With a bunch of grumbles, and what I could only assume were Rhonar curses, he eventually saw the error of his thinking. I wasn't too mad about it. If I was honest, it was nice having someone worry about me. I'd been independent for a long time, always fighting my way up the ladder and working toward my goals. So to have someone concerned about my health and happiness, not to mention my safety? Well, I didn't have it in me to complain about that.

"Fine," Xelan conceded at last. "But you'll do everything I, or Brok, says." He waved a finger at me, and I couldn't hold back the grin. "No arguments."

I grasped the hand of his waving finger and brought it to my chest. "I promise, Xelan. I just want to help." Holding his gaze, I added, "It's important to me."

He sighed. "I understand. I just…" He stepped closer, invading my space and kissing me deeply. His tongue rolled against mine, all his feelings apparent in his kiss. When he let me go, he put our foreheads together, and said, "I don't want anything to happen to you."

"Same, big guy!" I patted his cheek. "So let's make it through this together. Okay?"

He nodded. For about an hour—or span as they called it—we went over the plan. Tallis and Maena would stay behind. Brok had been posing as Xelan's bodyguard since the beginning, so his presence at a social event would be accepted, part of an Elite's security precautions. Since I was the newest "prize" as the Elites liked to name their favored slaves, Xelan would be showing me off. It meant changing from the lovely dress Maena had procured for me to an outfit that was…well, not lovely.

"Are you sure I should be wearing this?" I picked at the skintight material that had to be the Craxion version of latex.

Xelan's eyes narrowed. "You could always stay here."

"Nice try." I shook my head. "It's fine. I'll get used to it. At least it's not showing skin." The merlot-colored bodysuit covered me from neck to ankle and came with a matching pair of equally tight knee-high boots. The fabric was more functional than it appeared. Apparently, it would serve as insulation against Craxon's nightly frost and regulate my temperature. It also happened to show off every curve of my body, but it was full coverage—technically. *Small favors.*

As soon I was dressed and ready, Xelan strode toward the stairs, my hand tucked into the crook of his arm. It was as if he couldn't stand to break contact with me. That little voice popped up again, cautioning me that I should be concerned about his possessiveness. If we were back on Earth and he were human, I would be. But stuck on an alien planet as a slave? Not so much.

He did, however, let go as he went with Brok to procure our rides from the stables around back. What they brought forth nearly gave me a heart attack. "What is that thing?" I grimaced. It had six long legs and brown feathers, something like a cross between a camel, a horse, and a chicken.

"A catar," Brok said stoically, glancing around from where they'd brought the beasts. "We could get the carriage."

"No." Xelan waved toward the wide saddle atop one of the catar's backs. "She'll ride with me. It's faster than the carriage, and we may need that speed later."

Brok inclined his head. A drop of trepidation ran down my spine. *Will we need a quick getaway?* I thought it better not to ask.

With a blur of movement, Xelan lifted me onto the catar and jumped up behind me. His warm body pressed against my back. I tried to leave some room between us as the mating lust still claimed us hard—the evidence of it poking my ass—but he simply pulled me flush to him and growled in my ear. "No escaping."

I peeked over my shoulder as he used his free hand on the reins and kicked the creature into a trot. "I was trying to make us more comfortable." Shimmying in the saddle, I made my point clear as his cock grew impossibly harder. "See?"

He groaned. "Point taken."

A fraction of separation was all he allowed. I let loose a giggle. It was the most absurd thing to be on this planet, lusting after an alien, and now, on a mission to start a rebellion. If you would have told me that when I went into deep space, I'd end up like this, I would have gawked at the notion. Yet, somehow, it all felt right, like I was supposed to be here. I didn't know how it would turn out, but I couldn't regret the adventure.

Not until I saw the ominous and ultra weird mansion.

"What in all the stars above?" I gasped.

The ugliest building I'd ever seen stood framed by Craxon's dimming orange light as evening descended. It bathed the opulent monstrosity in rays of color that did nothing but enhance its hideousness. The mansion, as it had to be based on its sheer size, was asymmetrical. About three stories on one side, it teetered off to ground level on the other with a wide sloping roof. Spears that appeared jagged and sharp rose from the top. Windows, if they were windows, surrounded the structure in differing shapes: triangles, squares, diamonds, and long thin vertical rectangles. The glass was almost jet black, which matched the solid black walls, but each window had an illuminated frame in varying colors. There appeared no pattern to the windows as if a child had thrown around a bundle of blocks.

"It's the home of Denthar Calth, a Craxon Elite and host of this party," Xelan spoke through clenched teeth, and his body stiffened.

"It's quite…" I didn't have a word to describe the oddity that did it justice.

"Disgusting?" he finished for me.

"Yeah, that's true." I held onto Xelan's forearms as he helped me off the catar. "But I was thinking…creepy."

Brok took the reins of both creatures as we followed the narrow path to the house. When we reached the stone steps that led to the front door, he nodded at Xelan and went around the side of the building. Xelan glanced down at me. "He'll return. Since he's serving as my bodyguard he'll be expected to ensure our safety inside, but he needs to place the catars in a spot where they'll be easily accessible." He looped his arm through mine and held it tight. "Are you sure you want to do this?"

I straightened my spine, which stretched the skintight fabric I wore. But I answered, "Yes."

"Brave, Truxoria," he whispered to me and tucked a strand of hair behind my ear.

We climbed the short staircase, and Xelan grasped a golden ring attached to the enormous double doors. The doors were arched at the top and rose several feet, maybe a meter, above Xelan's head. As he slammed the ring against the door, it gave a gong that was loud enough to alert the entire household.

"Password?" an answering voice asked beyond the door.

Xelan procured the invitation which he had hidden under his armor. Staring at it, he pinched the bridge of his nose, and then said, "Elite pleasure. Elite demand."

The doors began to slide inward, revealing a silver metallic creature wearing a white vest and black trousers. "Thank you, sir."

I couldn't tell whether the butler was organic or robotic. His features were so unique, angular, and polished, he could have been either. But I didn't have long to ponder the servant's appearance as a massive beast straight out of my nightmares entered the front hall. His cloven feet were bare while the rest of him was covered in animal hide. A thick crimson cape rested across broad shoulders and gray scales. He was shorter than the Rhonar warriors, but four long horns jutted from his head. His lips thinned into a mockery of a smile.

I was sick to my stomach.

"Ah," the monster said. "My Rhonar friend, so good of you to come."

I went rigid and clung to Xelan's arm. My memories came crashing in, the whip handle flashing from beneath this beast's cloak as he stared at me with equal parts lust and anger. I shuddered and fought the urge to flee. The gray scaled, four-horned demon had returned. And this time, I couldn't run.

XELAN

Ava's fear wafted off her like spikes against my senses. The rage that it caused as I stared at this Craxion bastard was drav near impossible to shake off. I had to. I knew I had to. We had a party to get through and evidence to find, but I wanted to tear his head off and remove that sickening grin from his lips forever.

"Denthar Calth," I said through a tight jaw. I purposely left off his title to show that we were equals. "It's so kind of you to invite us."

"And is this the prize from the market?" His gaze locked on Ava, and it was more than I could handle as she continued to shake at my side.

"Indeed." I stepped in front of her, blocking his view. "And she's mine."

He laughed, an echoing noise like a boulder rolling off a cliff. "So possessive, dear Xelan. No matter. I hope you'll have a splendid time." He snapped his claws. "And Pizon told you of my gift? The new training device for our little slaves?"

"Oh yes." I took a step forward, hands fisted and ready to strike. "He most certainly did." My katra began to glow red, the power rising as fierce as wild fire. Crex the consequences! This bastard was going to pay. *NOW*.

"My Lord," a voice called behind me, but it sounded far away as my kedara rushed in my ears. "All is well with the perimeter, Lord Xelan." A restraining hand landed on my shoulder, and only then, did Brok's steadying calm pierce my rage-filled haze. "Where would you like me stationed?"

I studied him a beat. Brok's expression was passive enough to an outsider, but I knew his meaning. He wanted me to stand down. It took everything I had to push aside the rage. Calling on every facet of my warrior training, I choked back the anger, a painful gulp at a time. *The bastard's time will come,* I thought. It wasn't much consolation, but it kept me from ripping the Craxion's heart out.

"Your man should enjoy the party too. My security is top of the line." Calth waved at Brok. "No one goes anywhere without my knowledge. So your guard can relax." Not giving us a chance to respond, he swept his cloak to one side and spun on his hoofed heel. "Bafoo, give them a tour, and then, show them to the main stage. The entertainment will begin soon."

He left the foyer with a flourish, leaving his cybernetic butler to attend us.

"Are you all right?" I whirled to Ava, not caring that the droid, who was more robotic than organic, had already begun spinning his wheels toward a side hall.

Her breathing evened, but the fear clung to her. Yet she didn't waver as she held my gaze. "I can do this."

"I know you can, my mate." I palmed her cheek, so small and soft in my hand. "But you don't have to. Brok and I can handle it."

"No," she said firmly. Her tiny booted foot stamped in place. "Together, or not at all." With that, she followed behind the butler, forcing Brok and me to do the same.

I could have left right then. A part of me, the baser part, raged at me to do it. For a breath, I imagined picking her up, throwing her over my shoulder, and running out of there. What did I care about this drav planet, when my mate was at risk? But her rigid spine and purposeful stride gave me pause. She was determined to see this through, even battling her fear. My Truxoria was strong, and I would not make her weak with my own fears.

Catching up to her, I claimed her hand once more and placed it on my arm. "Together then."

Chapter 12

AVA

THE IMAGE OF THAT GRAY MONSTER PULLING THE WHIP from beneath his cloak would not leave me. I tried to push the memory away, holding Xelan's arm for strength, but it was still too fresh and raw in my mind. As we followed the robotic butler through the hallways, I sucked in a breath. My alien warrior could feel my emotions, and if I didn't want him terminating the mission, then I had to hold it together.

"What's this?" I pointed to a random door without caring about the answer. I just needed a distraction.

Bafoo the butler spun on his tiny wheels and came closer. "That's the study where Master Calth attends to matters regarding the Craxion Elite."

My brows rose to my hairline. I hadn't intended to discover any pertinent information with my question, but it seemed the universe was looking out for us. "That's fascinating."

Xelan nodded, glancing briefly at Brok behind us, before speaking to the butler. "And does Lord Calth keep records of all his affairs?"

Bafoo sputtered at that. "Why, of course, my Lord!" The man's pupils whirled in circles like a plastic pair of googly eyes. "My master is a fine businessman. He keeps impervious records."

"Assuredly." Xelan's answering smile was lost on the butler. "Brok, perhaps you should patrol these halls. If anyone was lurking about, surely, they'd be here."

"My word." The butler's tiny hands with stick thin arms fluttered like an orchestra conductor. "Our security is excellent. I would not think such a precaution necessary."

Stepping into the butler's personal space, Xelan used his substantial height to look down on the little guy. "But I do." It was all he needed to say.

"Yes, yes, certainly." His wheels spun once more as he motioned us forward. "As your lordship prefers."

Brok inclined his head, and then took a post two doors from the study. If anything was to be found there, with luck, he would find it, and we'd be able to leave this place. I hoped for that anyway as Xelan and I continued to follow the butler. He showed us a garden area, massive dining room, random living spaces, and such, until we arrived at what was described as the main stage.

Another set of double doors that mirrored the front pair opened into an interior rotunda. I gasped as we entered. "This is…" But I couldn't find the words to finish the sentence. The main stage, as the space was aptly named, had a circular platform in the center. Around it were placed chairs that looked more like ancient thrones. Black padding with gold inlay rested on the high-backed seats with an additional crimson pillow at the foot of each. At the far side, a throne slightly bigger than the rest had cushions all of gold.

As I stared in awe, other guests arrived. Most had gray scales and horns, but none were as large as Xelan. In fact, most were around my height, which, at an inch or so over five feet, wasn't large at all. They were shaped in every proportion from apple to pear to… *Is he broccoli shaped?* The male's head had clumps of hair around his horns and a long body that made him appear like the gray version of my least favorite vegetable. I shook my head at the sight.

"Come, Ava. Let's find our spot." Xelan guided me with a hand at the small of my back. The warmth from his palm helped to anchor me in the present. I didn't know how I would have handled the overwhelming urge to run without him. It grew stronger as Lord Calth entered the room.

"My Lords of Craxon," the beast announced as he ascended the main platform and spun in a circle, "and honored guests." He smiled down at Xelan. "Welcome to my home." Making a grand show of sweeping his cape over his shoulder like a bull fighter, he waved it at the thrones. "Please find your name and have a seat. The pillow at the base is for your lovely prizes."

I shuddered. The big Craxion was beyond creepy, but his use of the word "prizes" to describe people put him in the sociopath category. I didn't care if it was a Craxion Elite thing, it made them all messed up in my opinion.

Making our way to the assigned throne—and my pillow—I noticed the other females in the room. They varied in shape, size, and coloring. Most, in fact, had bright skin tones from a grass green alien with pink markings that appeared like flower petals on her skin to another who was an orange creamsicle shade with sunflower yellow hair. Most were dressed in thin fabric that left little to the imagination. Although my cat-suit may have been tight, I was thankful for the coverage.

The males began to take their seats while the females knelt on the pillows at their feet. I stared at mine for a heartbeat, willing my knees to bend. *It's a show. Just pretend. You can do this.* But no matter how I framed it, my mind wouldn't allow it. Every woman in that room was a slave, owned, used, and abused by these powerful, arrogant lords. I couldn't make myself one of them.

"Ava?" Xelan's voice roused me from my tumultuous thoughts. He must have sensed the war within me because he leaned over and whispered in my ear, "Would you kneel for me, my Truxoria?" His scent invaded my senses, the decadent chocolate with a hint of spice. "Not for any of these bastards, and not because you're less than them." He gripped my chin, gently turning my head so our eyes locked. "Would you kneel because I asked you to?" His forehead rested against mine, and his hand slid to my back to pull me flush with his body. "Because I demanded it?"

Fuck. Suddenly, I wasn't in that room anymore. I was floating and melting at the same time, lost at sea in waves of lust that were all for my alien, for Xelan. *Yes,* I thought deliriously. Without further worrying, I knelt on the pillow, and he sat on the throne. He bent over to guide my arms around his legs and to wrap his fingers in my hair.

"Together," he said to me, then leaned against the high-backed seat. His hand stayed in my hair, and mine remained around his leg.

It was an odd feeling, a dichotomy of emotions as I had never felt so safe, loved, and—although I barely could believe it—respected, while being in a place of such depravity and danger. Unfortunately, it didn't last. A gong pervaded the momentary peace, louder even than the one that had announced our arrival. I winced at the noise and Xelan's muscles tightened under my hands.

"It is time to begin!" Lord Calth shouted from center stage. The lights went out at his announcement, plunging the room in darkness. Shuffles and grumbles could be heard from all directions.

Xelan moved his hand to my face as if needing the reassurance I was still there. I hugged his leg harder.

A dim red glow began to emanate from the edge of the ring. Slowly, it grew brighter until a lone figure was silhouetted on the platform. A woman with elegant curves and long legs was bathed in the red light. Her fiery hair shifted on her head like living flames, and her skin was as blue as a forget-me-not flower. Black scarves wrapped around her breasts while another draped over her hips to fall between her legs. She wore thigh-high boots with sharp pointed heels. A spotlight flashed onto the stage and it moved about the platform. The alien woman flowed with it, dancing in a style that was beautiful and sad at the same time.

I held my breath. She was as graceful as any ballerina, but the dance was so utterly foreign, so alien, and yet, it struck a cord in me. Her perfect lines and coordinated turns made it seem like she danced through water. A haunting melody played from unseen speakers and changed the feel of the room. A moody hush enveloped the crowd.

When the song ended and the woman stopped her dance, a single clap echoed in the robust space. "My sweet one," Lord Calth, now perched on his golden throne, rose and spoke to her. "What a lovely dance you gave us."

She dropped to her knees immediately and bowed her head.

The gray monster walked toward the platform. A set of stairs were mounted on one side of the circle, and he strode toward them on his horrible hoofed feet like a king about to give court. The thump of his steps was a weight on my heart. Something awful was about to happen. I could sense it in my bones.

"Ava," Xelan called to me, tugging at my hair to get my attention. "Come up here and sit in my lap. Now."

He must have the same thoughts as I did. Then again, he could feel the emotions of others, so he must know, even more than me, that something was off. I scrambled from the cushion and into Xelan's lap. I didn't even think about arguing, wanting to be closer to him as a thickness clogged my throat.

"Truxoria," he whispered in my hair. His arms wrapped tight around me. "When I tell you, I want you to bury your head in the crook of my neck. Understand?"

I blinked up at him. "Why?"

"I'll explain later." The tension in his words left no room for discussion.

As the intensity in the space increased, I watched the scene unfold with clenched fists. Lord Calth had stood within arms length of the woman. His sharp claws reached for her hair and dragged her to her feet. His free hand traced the delicate skin of her throat. "Such an exquisite prize, you are." With infinite slowness he ran one pointed claw over her breasts and down her arm. When he reached her hand, he hissed, "But so disobedient."

In a flash of movement, the monster reached inside his cloak and locked a manacle around her wrist. Swiftly, he locked its counterpart on her opposite wrist and strung them from a hook that had descended from the ceiling. He did the same to her ankles, shackling them and hooking the contraption to grates that rose from the floor.

"What is this?" I spun to face Xelan, horrified at the display on stage.

"Easy, Ava." His hand landed in my hair again. "Remember what I said."

I whirled back to the stage, unable to look away. The spotlight brightened to show the poor woman chained and shaking. That sicko was circling her like a predator toying with its prey. "Now, my guests, see what my new device can do with an unruly slave, such as this." He motioned to the woman and reached inside his cloak once more. I only got a glimpse of the device, before Xelan spun my whole body into his chest. Forcefully, though not painfully, he pushed my face into the crook of his neck.

But that small flash was all I needed.

"Xelan," I cried on the verge of tears. "We can't let this happen."

"My mate," he spoke at my ear, the warmth of his breath on my neck, "if there were anyway I could prevent it, I would." His grip tightened, not allowing me to move when I started to squirm. "If we intervene, we'll be caught, and the mission will be over."

"I don't care," I sobbed. My tears flowed freely now as I heard the crackling of the electric whip. "I don't want anyone to suffer like I did."

"I know." He held me somehow yet closer, even though I rested in his lap, my side against his chest and my face at his neck. "You're kind and good and everything that should be far, far away from this crexing planet." His nose pushed at my hair, nuzzling the strands. "I'd damn the mission and save the female, but I cannot, I *will* not risk you. I will not compromise your safety for any reason. Do you understand?"

A hiccup came forth, and the woman's cries reached my ears. The sobs lodged in my throat. "N-no, I c-can't accept that."

"I'm sorry, Ava." He clasped his hand over my ear, pushing the other against his chest. It effectively blocked out the noise while keeping my face turned away from the awful scene on the stage.

I wanted to fight him, to tell him that we had to save the woman. But fear gripped me. As I pictured that woman's terror and the horrors that befell her on that platform, for a moment, our places were reversed. It was me center stage, bound and chained, and beaten with electrified lashes. I sobbed harder.

Xelan held me through it all, never allowing me to glimpse the scene further. "It's almost over, my love."

Liquid warmth infused me as I heard him utter the word *love* for the first time. I wanted to revel in that sensation and wrap it around me like a blanket. But the horror show kept playing through my mind, and I knew that although I hadn't witnessed it with my eyes, my body would remember the trauma. And I'd be playing over this night in my head for a long time to come.

Chapter 13

XELAN

I SHOULD HAVE NEVER BROUGHT HER ON THE MISSION. IT was a terrible idea. As that poor female on the stage suffered the whips from that bastard, Ava's body shook in response. Every lash was one that had been done to my mate, every cry from the female's lips had been uttered by my Truxoria. If I thought I experienced rage before, it was nothing to how I felt now.

I'll kill him. It was a threat and a vow rolled into one. Before I left this drav planet, I would eliminate that Craxion. I glared in hatred. If anyone looked at me now, they would see it plain on my face. But all eyes were fixed on the stage.

After far too long, it ended. The female was released and dragged off the platform by two servants, similar in appearance to the butler.

"I hope you have enjoyed the entertainment, my friends." Calth had the audacity to bow. "And now, the bidding for one of my new toys," he held up the handle of the whip, the crackles of the lashes still stinging with electricity, "shall begin."

I'd had enough. Talking softly in Ava's ear, I said, "We're leaving."

"No," she cried, fisting her small hands on my armor. "We can't go yet. We need," a residual hiccup from her sobs bubbled forth, "the evidence."

"Then, we'll help Brok find it." I stood, keeping her in my arms and tight against my chest where she belonged.

She swatted at me. "I can walk, you know."

"Not right now." I needed her body close to mine, her breath on my skin. She was the only thing keeping me from losing control. And yet, it was for her that I wanted so badly to let go and destroy every single one of those sick bastards.

"Okay." She sighed, rubbing her cheek against my collarbone. "I don't really want you to let me go anyway."

I smiled at that. My brave Truxoria had the courage of a warrior, but I relished her confession. To the world, she would be hard and fierce, but for me, she would be soft and yielding. It was the perfect combination, and I knew for certain, she was destined to be mine.

And I to be hers.

The thought anchored me enough to finish the job. For if I allowed my anger to take over, then she would be put in danger. And that was unacceptable.

Passing the Craxion Elites who were bidding on that disgusting torture device, I noticed the faces of the females. A few held notes of fear, but most, almost all, wore expressions of resolve. It turned my kedara cold. No one should be made to suffer in such a manner, but especially not females. They were meant to be cherished. I'd been taught that before my ascent to malehood and believed it all through my time battling the hunger and then the void. But now, having been given back my emotional core, thanks to my mate, I felt it in the deepest parts of my soul.

"Xelan?" Ava's questioning stare had me moving faster.

I could do nothing for the females now, but once we completed this mission, they would be one step closer to freedom. "It's all right." I held her tight, wanting nothing more than to shield her from all of the madness around us. "Let's finish this."

We left through the double doors, the only exit from the rotunda, without anyone stopping us. The others were too fixated on the auction to notice our departure. Once we rounded the attached hallway, Ava stirred. "You can put me down now. It's better if I walk from here." She glanced around. "In case you need your hands."

True. If we happened upon anyone who questioned our presence, well, a fight was a likely result. And I would need my hands free. "You're right."

Setting her on the ground, I waited a beat for her to settle and straighten. She smiled at me. "All good."

I didn't believe that for an instant, but neither would I deny her spirit. I nodded, taking her hand in mine. The hallways were purposefully misleading as if built to trap one inside. But the Craxion had not accounted for my kind. The Rhonar had long developed skills for combat, but our abilities did not end on the battlefield. Spatial awareness, adaptive memory, and keen observation were useful in a conflict—and for tactical means. A warrior's mind for strategy was as valuable, if not more so, than his strength.

With confidence I had memorized the route, I led us back to the hallway where we had discovered the study and Brok stood guard. The corridor was empty. Cautiously, I tugged Ava to my side as I scanned the door of the study. It was cracked open. I peered inside, searching the interior.

"Any sign of Brok?" Ava whispered, close on my heels.

"I don't see him." I pushed the door open a bit wider. Two wall sconces on the farthest side of the room provided only a small margin of light. A diamond shaped window with black glass allowed for little more. Narrowing my eyes, I tried to see if anything threatening awaited us. A large desk, constructed of an obsidian substance, took up the majority of the space. Atop it sat a curved screen and holo-keys. Behind it was a high-backed chair similar to the ones in the main stage, but it had no padding and seemed to be made of the same material as the desk. The walls held no ornamentation or decoration. They too were solid black.

"This is a study?" Ava scoffed, lifting my arm and peering from under it. "Who could focus in here?"

I shrugged.

Inching closer, she put one hand on my waist and the other gripped my thigh. My thoughts turned molten. "Ava," I warned.

"What?" she asked innocently, then glanced at the obvious issue. Her fingers rested dangerously close to the bulge beneath my leathers. "Oh." The rose hue, that I had fast become addicted to, warmed her cheeks. "Sorry." To my chagrin, she moved her hand away.

Focusing on the task at hand, and sensing no obvious danger, I guided her into the study. Even in the dim light, I could tell Brok wasn't there. I'd worry about finding him after we checked the desk. I detected no other emotions in the vicinity beside Ava's and mine. "Let's see if we can access Calth's files." I pointed to each of the drawers on the slick surface, showing Ava where to push them to pop them open, and then leaving her to search through them. I concentrated on the holo-keys.

It took a surprisingly short time to crack the code on the encryption. I wasn't even the best at tech out of my Rhonar brathers, having a rudimentary understanding of security systems at best. *I shouldn't have been able to do this so easily.* Warning alarms blared in my mind, but I kept my attention on the Craxion's holo-files. I was a mere handful in, before I found what we'd been searching for.

"Crex," I muttered. Holo-vids and docs popped up, depicting the movements of the Craxion Elite. From abuse and torture of their slaves, to back-alley deals in illegal wares, to the corrupt transactions where power traded hands for political, economic, or financial gain. It was all the proof we needed, and it was right at my fingertips. I reached under my armor for the flash key hidden there.

"What is all this?" Ava's hushed tone had me moving faster.

"Evidence." It was all I said as I worked quickly to copy the files to the storage device.

"Look at this," she cried as she held up a rounded piece of metal from the interior drawer. Less the length of her pink, it bore Calth's seal on the end. "And there's letters inside."

I kept copying the digital files, willing the machine to move faster. "Put it all inside my armor. We can sort it later."

Doing as I asked, she stuffed the letters and the seal beneath my chest plate, her small hand brushing my skin. My anxiety spiked, despite the comfort of her touch. Time was against us, as I sensed a trap closing. "Ava, I want you to head for the front door."

She took a step back, her startled emotions pushing against my senses. "What? Why?"

"Truxoria." I didn't turn to her, but I kept the seriousness in my tone. "Go now."

But it was too late. The files finished copying, and I shoved the flash key beneath my armor with the rest of the evidence, as the emotions of others battered my empathic shields. I felt them before they arrived. Pushing Ava behind me, I crept along the wall. The study had only one entrance, and therefore, one exit.

"Xelan, what is it?" She kept behind me, holding tight to my waist.

"Company." I wanted to hold her, to tell her it would be all right. But I didn't dare to take my gaze from the door. I had no weapons. As a guest in the home of a Craxion Lord, I knew I'd be allowed none. Although I missed my sword and knives, I didn't need them. I was the weapon.

Two Craxion guards entered first, curved blades in their hands. They were shorter than me and less broad, but not as minuscule as the Craxion Elite, and no less dangerous for their smaller stature. I never underestimated an enemy. Calth entered after them, his crimson cloak dragging behind him.

"Ah, dear Xelan, and how intriguing to find you here." His thin-lipped grin made him appear like a gray gekgoid lizard, basking in the sun.

I didn't bother with a defense. He'd set the trap, and I'd walked into it.

"We were just looking for some privacy," Ava provided, but her explanation would not appease the likes of that crexer.

"Privacy, you say?" The bastard tried to peer around me to her.

That wasn't happening. I blocked her with my body and kept her firmly behind me.

"Yes?" She likely meant it to be a statement, but it sounded too much like a question.

"I see." Calth stroked his angular chin with his claws. "Well, it seems you've had quite enough time for your privacy together." His black eyes locked on mine. "I think I'd like some private time with her now."

I growled. The hair on the back of my neck rose and my jaw locked tight. "Never."

"Then, we're at an impasse." The bastard hummed. "Of course, I could claim *salgar ludayam*. My guests would enjoy another show."

I held back my laugh, but not the grim smile. "You want to challenge me to blood sport?" It was the official Craxion words for a challenge of combat. I'd heard it uttered many times in the streets of the slave markets, where battles over prized slaves often occurred.

"Yes, Xelan," he pointed over my shoulder, "for a prize."

My teeth ground together. I wasn't in doubt I could defeat him, but to put Ava's freedom on the line? If I lost by chance, or if the draving Craxion cheated his way to victory, she would suffer for it. I didn't fear death, but her life was far more precious.

"I won't bargain with her."

"Would you rather I kill you both now?" The guards at his sides thrust their blades. "That is the price for trespassing, after all."

"No!" Ava slid around me, facing the guards. "I'm willing."

Grabbing her and spinning around, I put my back to the Craxions with their drawn weapons. It wasn't my wisest move, but seeing her in danger and offering herself up as a prize drove me half mad. "What are you doing?"

"Xelan," she put her delicate hand on my neck, "I trust you." Her eyes narrowed as she peered over my shoulder. "And you can beat him. If you don't take his offer, they'll kill you." Those beautiful brown eyes turned back to me. "I can't let that happen."

My stomach churned. The icy blades of fear slithered through me at the risk of losing her. But what choice did I have? I might be able to take out Calth and his guards here, but could I do so without Ava being harmed in the process? I wasn't sure. Holding her hand against my neck, I tugged her to me. My hearts beat hard behind my ribs for her. *Always for her.* Not caring that we had an audience, I took her lips in a blazing kiss. I pushed all of my emotions into it, so she would know that no matter what happened, she was mine.

"What a touching display." Calth sneered. His guards shifted beside him, chuckling. "It will be so delicious to take her from you."

I whirled around, faster than I knew the bastard could track, and invaded his space. The guards may have had blades, but I was quicker, and the Craxions had to step back. "I'll agree to your challenge," I barked. My fists clenched and unclenched in rapid succession. "But I want my bodyguard as my second. Find him." If Calth had captured Brok, he would need to let him go to fulfill the requirements of the *salgar ludayam*. Every combatant was entitled to a second to oversee that the match was fair.

"Oh no, have you lost your male-servant?" His tongue clacked against his lower fangs. "How unfortunate."

I snarled. "No games, Calth. Procure my brather, or the blood sport will begin here and now." The balls of my feet dug into the ground beneath me as I prepared to attack.

His dark laughter filled the cramped space. "Heel, Rhonar glack. You'll have the male."

Rage stormed in my gut, expanding to my limbs. The insult he spat at me added kindling to the fire inside me. I trusted Brok to defend himself, but he was still a lone warrior, and I'd left him. Before I did something rash, Ava put a steadying hand on my hip.

"Together," she whispered for my ears alone.

Her sweet voice was like a spring rain on my internal inferno, gently dousing the flames so I could think again. She gave me back the same promise I had made to her, and it steeled my resolve. I would find my brather, save my mate, and set a spark to the rebellion.

Before another solar day passed on this planet, the Craxion Elite would burn to ash.

Chapter 14

AVA

FEAR TURNED MY MUSCLES TO JELLY, MY INSIDES LIKE A limp noodle. I could not remember ever being so afraid. Even staring at that gray monster for the first time, or waking up in a cage, or seeing the flash of the whip, didn't compare. Certainly nothing in my life back on Earth had prepared me for watching the male I loved fight in a death match.

Wait? Loved?

My breath caught. When or how it happened, I didn't know, but the feeling was real. Although it hadn't been long, it felt like I'd known him forever. *Is that what it means to be mates?* His people believed in fated mates, those destined to be together by some universal design. It was hard to wrap my head around the idea, and the closest we had on Earth was soul mates. But I'd never been one to buy into all that. I was an academic, a scientist. *With crystals on your desk at home.* Yeah, but they were pretty. *And a manifestation journal in the drawer.* That was promoting positivity. Oh hell, what was I even thinking about?

I loved the big alien. Plain and simple. Maybe it was irrational, or maybe it was destiny. It didn't matter. All that did was he survived this madness—and we could be together. Like it or not, free or not, I wanted that. I wanted to be with him.

"You can do it," I shouted as he stepped onto the platform back in the main stage area. The Craxion Elites had finished their auction, and now, with the promise of this match, they were sitting forward in their seats. I stood near the door where Xelan had told me to remain. If things went bad, he wanted me close to the exit.

Glancing back at me, he shot me a confident half-grin. Then, his focus turned to the center of the stage. "Where is my second?" he barked in a booming voice.

From the other side of the platform, two guards brought forth a chained figure. Before the spotlight hit him, I knew it was Brok. The way Xelan's hands fisted and his back went rigid was proof enough. "Free him." Lord Calth snapped his claws and motioned to the guards. "Let him stand as second for my opponent."

The manacles on Brok's wrists dropped to the ground with a loud thud. He rubbed them but showed no other hint of pain or discomfort. His hair, which I had only ever seen tied at the nape of his neck, was loose around his shoulders and matted. Dried blood and a lump at the back of his head were evident, even from across the room. He walked forward with purposeful steps. Spying me, he nodded, and then made his way toward the stairs at the side of the platform. Ascending them, he clasped forearms with Xelan. Whatever words they shared were for their ears alone. Then, Brok took position at a spot directly in line with me on the platform and crossed his arms over his massive chest. My stomach rolled. He wasn't just watching out for Xelan, he was stationing himself closer to me. I could tell from the glances that the warriors shared between them and how their eyes cut to me.

I would not cry. Damn it.

Both of these males were so brave and honorable. More than anyone I'd ever known. If my eyes got a little watery, well, that was that. But I was not letting the tears fall. I had to buck up my courage, especially for Xelan. "You're going to win," I whispered, willing it to be true.

And if the universe had put us together, then no one was tearing us apart.

The gong that I had come to hate in such a short time rung again. Three Craxion guards stood on the platform on the gray beast's side. The two aliens circled the platform, never showing their back to the other. Xelan walked slowly, casually, as if he were not in a fight for his life. Lord Calth, on the other hand, was hunched over slightly, his claws held out in front of his chest. He kept his crimson cloak on, which I thought odd. *Who battles in a cloak?* Before I could ponder the question, the monster launched across the ring.

I sucked in air through my teeth. Xelan dodged him, letting the monster's momentum carry him to the edge of the platform. He capitalized on that movement by spinning and landing a devastating kick to the middle of that crimson cloak. Lord Calth howled.

"You nasty ghit," the gray beast shouted as he flicked off his cloak and threw it to the ground below. "I'll make you pay for that."

Xelan didn't respond with words, instead he stood tall and stared down his opponent.

Lord Calth charged again, but Xelan didn't dodge this time. My heart leapt into my throat, and I absently massaged the spot on my neck. Locking his hands around gray forearms, my alien warrior used the asshole's body weight and force from the charge to throw him to the ground. The monster landed on his back, staring up at the spotlight overhead.

"Yield now, and end this, Calth." Xelan's words rang clear for all to hear.

My eyes widened in shock. I knew what it meant for him to make such an offer. It was obvious Xelan was the superior fighter, but he had wanted to kill that gray monster. Hell, a part of me did too for everything I'd suffered. But for that asshole to be so outmatched didn't feel fair, even if he deserved death.

Admiration for my mate filled me. If we had the chance to build a life together, I wondered how that would continue to grow and what other ways he might still surprise me. I wanted that. I wanted that so badly I could taste it.

"Please," I said aloud, not knowing to whom I was speaking. But whatever higher powers might exist I hoped they'd hear me. "Let this end soon. And give us a chance."

XELAN

I wanted to crush him right there in the center of the ring. The bastard had been the scourge of Craxon, the center of the corruption, since we'd first landed on this crexing planet. He had caused more suffering than anyone. He didn't deserve mercy, only death.

Yet something held me back.

The slithering sensation of unease tingled my spine. Feelings battered my shields: Calth's anger, the onlooker's macabre curiosity and bloodthirsty desire, and Ava's fear and awe. It wasn't any of them that stayed my hand from making the kill. No, it was me. I felt...*Empathy?*

I had never considered how my emotions would play into a battle, only those of my opponents. I had used them as a weapon. An enemy's fear could make them run when they should strike or anger cloud their judgment. It didn't occur to me that having feelings of my own would change the nature of my fighting—or doling out death. I wasn't opposed to killing when I needed to; even now, I knew strategically that it was the right course. For what he'd done to Ava alone, Calth needed to die.

But still, I'd give him this one chance, just one, to save his wretched hide. I glared down at him. "What say you?"

"Mercy from a Rhonar warrior?" He sneered, rising to his knees. "How very droll."

"I'll have no trouble killing you after this, you crexer." I readied into a fighting stance, no longer toying with this fool. "You have one chance to live. Yield or die."

Calth rose to his full height, waving a hand at me as he did. "No need for such dramatics. You're clearly the victor." The strain around his thin lips didn't match his words, nor did the ire rolling off him.

"You yield then?" I asked, suspicion evident in my tone. I didn't drop my guard.

He turned his back to me. "Yes, yes. I yield."

Groans of disappointment emanated from the crowd. A *salgar ludayam* could end in such a way, but it was unusual for the barbaric planet. I tried to tamper my own frustration. Wanting to end that drav bastard for good warred with my new feelings of fair play.

I didn't like it a bit.

"Then, this is settled." Motioning for Brok to follow me, I headed toward the platform's edge. "We're leaving."

Calth remained where he was, but the guards at his side suddenly drew blasters from their belts.

"What is this?" Brok asked before I could. He stood next to me now, his face a stoic mask.

A sense of excitement drew around the room. The Craxion bastard came to stand in front of us, his guards staying just behind him. "I admit Xelan that the *salgar ludayam* was a bit of a rouse. A way to lure you here." He purred the words, satisfaction rolling off him. "The real battle you see is this." Sweeping his claws forward in an elaborate motion, he said, "Kill them."

Brok and I needed no communication between us. Without sparing a second, I dropped into a fighting stance once more and Brok constructed his energy shield. He might not have been able to bring his trusted battle ax, but like all Rhonar, he had a unique ability. And his energy shield had saved us more than once. As the guards fired their blasters at us, it seemed it would again. "Stay within the shielding," he said to me as his katra glowed blue and the shield projected around us like a dome of protection. "Don't let them get a shot at you."

"Not a worry," I shouted, relishing the chance to battle with my brother. "They're no match for us." The guards' blasters would run out of charge long before

Brok's shielding. Seeming to sense this, the fire grew less, and their agitation increased.

"I'll move us closer, so the real fun can begin." Brok might not have felt joy, but even without emotions, he appreciated a good fight.

My kedara sang, my life's blood soaring through me. This was the heart of a Rhonar warrior. I had given my enemy a chance at mercy, and he spat it back in my face. I had nothing to feel now but the desire for blood and victory. My katra flared red.

It was time.

More Craxion guards piled onto the platform. Calth stood at the center, hands on his hips, and a maniacal grin on his face. He was my target. "Get us as close as you can to that bastard," I murmured to Brok. "But leave him to me."

Brok grunted.

When the guards realized we were gaining ground, they tried to back away. But the platform prevented them from fleeing too far. Once in fighting distance, we engaged. A strike at the throat here, a twist of a head there, and they fell at our feet one after the other. It took little time before a mere handful remained.

Calth lost confidence, heading for the stairs. The crowd chanted their displeasure.

"Go, I've got this." Brok motioned for me to leave as he turned toward the remaining guards.

I trusted his word and headed after the cowardly lord. He fled like a male possessed, screaming at the Craxion Elite to get out of his way. I closed the distance between us faster than he could escape. "Face me, Calth!"

He hissed and spun on his hoofed feet. "Come closer, and she dies." He pointed a sharp claw in Ava's direction, but he was too far from her. His desperation reeked.

"Enough!" I struck him hard in the gut.

Bowing in half, he coughed up black blood. A swift knee to the face had him grabbing his flat nose. I didn't let up —a series of jabs to the throat and chest, then a good kick to his hip. He went down hard, and still I didn't relent. His gurgling noises told me he was fading, but he dug his claws into my calf. The pain radiated up my thigh, but I ignored it. Calth would not get away. He'd pay for all of the atrocities he committed with his life. I'd see to that.

A soft flowery scent filled my nose, surpassing the rancid battle aromas. *Ava.*

In the heat of the fight I had not thought of her, much to my shame. Her safety was above all else. She pushed through the crowd, standing across from me. Our eyes locked. Hers were glassy, but she held her head high. *My brave Truxoria.*

As I stared at her, I didn't notice the movement from Calth until it was too late. A vial crashed against my leg where he'd first marked me with his claws. The liquid inside seeped into my broken skin. "Nah-ow," he gurgled over a mouth full of blood, "weh bahth duh-ai."

His black eyes rolled back and his head lolled to the side. Calth was dead. But whatever he used against my wounded calf stung more than a swarm of hornrills. My katra dimmed. Worse I felt the foreign substance move through my blood, burning as it went. I fell to one knee.

Ava screamed.

I longed to hold her. If my life ended here, I needed to feel her in my arms a final time. Reaching for her, I saw two, then three of her. Every one of her stretched their arms through the crowd. I brushed the fingertips of the middle Ava, before the ground began to rise and hit me in the face.

With a crashing finality, my world plunged into darkness.

Chapter 15

AVA

"Xelan! Xelan!" The cries poured out of me. Pain seared my chest as if my heart were trying to break through my ribcage. I pushed and shoved the aliens beside me. The vulgar males had packed together when the fighting began, all jockeying for a better view. When I at last reached Xelan, he was face down on the ground. His breath hissed low and labored.

"Help!" I screamed over the throng. "Someone please, help!"

I scanned the crowd. Brok was still on the platform, fighting off the remaining guards. A bubble of pure energy surrounded him and the markings on his arms glowed blue. He couldn't help now. I continued to search for aid. "Please, anyone!"

Sensing the show was over, the Craxion assholes ignored my pleas and began to file from the room. A sob escaped me. I couldn't lose it. I had to get help. Stiffening my lip,

I kept looking among the aliens for a friendly face—or at least a neutral one. The female slaves had mostly gone with their masters, but a few outcasts were lingering at the back. I recognized one as the dancer from earlier.

Her golden eyes bore into mine before she turned them toward Lord Calth, who stayed unmoving several paces from where Xelan lay. She let loose a growl, then set her gaze to me again. She nodded. Thick material, that might have been bandages, was wrapped around her shoulders, torso, and although I couldn't see, I guessed her back too. Yet, her steps when walking were as fluid and graceful as her dance had been. She strode toward me. "Is he dead then?"

For a heartbeat, I thought she meant Xelan, and I nearly lunged at her. But then, she inclined her head toward the gray monster.

I spared a moment to analyze Lord Calth's prone form. I didn't know for sure, but I wasn't about to tell her that, so I said, "He's dead."

"Good." She knelt by Xelan's other side across from me. "I'm Jadara. And your master has been poisoned."

"He's…" The sob that I had been trying so hard to hold back escaped. "H-he's n-not my m-master." I bit my lip and sucked in a steadying breath through my nose. "He's my mate."

Thick red lashes fluttered as she blinked. "Your mate? But he's an Elite."

In a spur of the moment decision, I determined it was better to reveal Xelan's identity than keep up the facade. If he was poisoned as Jadara claimed, then it wouldn't matter anyway. "He's undercover. He has been from the start." I held tight to his arm, willing him to hang on. "He's not an Elite. He's a Rhonar warrior, and he's trying to help."

Her blue nostrils flared, and I could tell she didn't believe me.

"It's true!" I cried, racking my brain for a way to convince her. "We were here gathering evidence, and we found some."

"You found evidence for what?" She sat back on her heels, scrutinizing me.

"Well…" I tried to gauge how much I could trust her, but Xelan's harsh breathing was making me frantic. "It's for the rebellion, to convince the holdouts and gain them the numbers they need to win."

Her answering smile lit up her face. "If that's the case, then we're on the same side."

It was then Brok descended the platform and rushed to us. "Is he?"

Jadara answered, "He's been poisoned with paerana root. He needs the antidote or he'll die."

"How do you know this?" Brok's growl of warning beneath his words was deadly. Had I been on its receiving end, I would have cowered. Jadara didn't even flinch.

"I've been with this glack for more cycles than I can count." She spat at Lord Calth's body. "I know which weapons he prefers. And paerana root poison is his favorite."

I reached across Xelan and grabbed her hand. "And the antidote? Do you know it?"

She stared at where my hand wrapped around hers, but she didn't pull away. "Are you really helping the rebellion?"

"Yes," Brok said without hesitation. "We are."

Her exhale was like that of someone who had held their breath for too long. "Then, I'll get you the antidote." She lifted her hand from my grip and held up two fingers like a scout's salute. "That is, if you give me the evidence you say you collected."

"But why?" I'd give her anything at all to save Xelan, but I didn't understand why she'd want it.

"You were gathering the evidence for the rebellion, right?" She jut out her chin and her fiery red hair danced atop her head like it had a mind of its own.

"That's correct." Brok crouched down, although with his height he still towered over us.

"Then, it's a fair trade. An antidote for the evidence." Jadara stuck a thumb to her chest. "Because you found a rebel."

I RECALLED THE EXIT FROM THE MAIN STAGE LIKE A dream, half remembered and blurry. Nothing had quite felt real. It was as if I had been moving through thick mud and my mind struggled to catch up. The weird robot butler, Bafoo, had entered in a fury, cleaning and sweeping at the bodies. When he'd tried to put a broom to Xelan, I'd sprung at him. Brok had pulled me off as I cursed, then he picked up Xelan and placed him over his shoulder. The Rhonar warrior was strong, but my mate was not a small male. It didn't seem to matter to Brok.

We followed Jadara through back hallways, clearly meant for servants or slaves. She guided us to a room that was out of the way from the rest. It had stone walls and a single pallet with a worn blanket on the floor. "Put him there," she motioned to it. "I'll need to go to the kitchens to fetch the ingredients and brew the antidote."

Brok placed Xelan gently atop the pallet with its sad blanket and glanced at me. "You can help him, Ava." He squeezed his friend's forearm, then took my hand and put it on the spot where he had squeezed. "Keep him with us. Talk to him, hold him, anchor him to the present." He tapped my fingers where they rested on

Xelan's skin. "You're his mate. Give him a reason to live."

I blinked the tears from my eyes and nodded. I'd do everything in my power to keep Xelan here. "I will."

"I'm going with Jadara to get those ingredients." He waved at the door. "We'll be back soon. Don't let him leave us."

"Never," I said fiercely and meant it.

When the door closed behind them, the full impact of Brok's words hit me. No matter what, I would keep my mate with me. I just had to figure out how.

Feeling his muscles under my fingers, I caressed him slowly back and forth. His beautiful bronze skin was cold to the touch. *Maybe that's where to start.* If my alien was cold, then I would warm him up. *The same as he did for me.* I found the clasps to his armor under his armpits and at his hips. I undid them, tugging on the weight of the material, which was surprisingly light, and cast the chest piece aside. Even in illness, Xelan was a work of art. Another time, after he lived through this—and he would live through this, I swore it—I would worship that masterpiece with my mouth.

Jerking my arms free of the tight latex-like cat-suit, I shoved it to my waist and exposed my breasts. I didn't care about the partial nudity. Xelan needed my warmth, and damn it, he was going to get it. I sat astride his trim waist, then carefully stretched atop him. I made sure to cover as much of his chest and torso as possible to keep those vital organs underneath warm. When my skin made contact with his, he groaned. It wasn't a pained sound either, but one of deep pleasure. I sighed in relief and hugged his sides.

"Xelan?" I stared at his face. His mouth was pinched. Lines creased his forehead. I wasn't deterred. "I can't wait to hear all about your people. I'm so curious to know more about the Rhonar." He remained silent, but a line or two appeared to soften on his brow. "Humans, that's what we call ourselves on Earth, are complicated. We waged wars against each other for centuries, all but destroyed our planet, and eventually, came together under a global government." Xelan's chest rose and fell beneath me, a sign that he was still with me. "Not everyone accepted it, of course, and some people are scared to death of technology. But they live in the outlands now. Sadly, there's only a few places left on Earth that are inhabitable anymore. Everything else was decimated by geographic shifts after our atmosphere partially collapsed."

I searched his features for any hint that he heard me. "I know that's all boring, right?" I didn't think so, but most people did. "I was actually on Earth's first deep space flight. I was tired of being the stuffy academic, you know? I wanted an adventure." I laughed without mirth. "Guess, I got one."

"Are you sorry?" His lids cracked open, those impossibly blue eyes staring at me.

"Xelan?" I didn't dare believe it. "Is this real? Are you with me?"

He hummed and the sound vibrated where our chests met.

"Oh." I burrowed in closer to him, hugging his middle tight. "Just stay with me. They're getting you an antidote, so you'll be all right. Hang in there."

"I'm not leaving you, Truxoria." He lifted his arm as if to reach for me, but it flopped at his side. He winced.

"Don't try to move." I rubbed his shoulder.

He sighed. "You didn't answer me."

"Huh?" I met his gaze.

"About having your space adventure. Are you sorry that you left Earth?" The doubt in his eyes was equal measure with hope. And it struck me that he didn't know how I felt about him.

"Xelan," I scooted up his chest, careful not to put too much strain on his body, "I've seen horrors on this planet, endured suffering and pain." His brow drew low at my words, as if he would rise and kill anyone who dared harm me again. That should have frightened me. I saw firsthand what that type of damage he could do. Yet all I felt was protected, safe. "But I would do it all again to be by your side."

A look of wonder lit his face. "Truly?"

"Yes." I couldn't hold back any longer. Sealing my lips to his, I poured myself into the kiss. Everything I felt, everything we still had yet to learn about each other, to say to one another, was expressed in that moment. My fear that he wouldn't survive mixed with my wish for a future together. All of it meshed as our tongues danced.

His body surged forward, bucking us into a reclining position, as if our mutual rising desire could eliminate the poison. But it was short-lived. We flopped back to the pallet with a thump.

"Xelan, I'm so sorry. I didn't mean for that to happen." I rushed off him. Then, I took the blanket from under him, frantically wrapping it around any exposed parts.

"Truxoria," he said, calling me again by the beautiful word I'd come to cherish. "Settle, I'm all right."

"No, you're not." My voice shook. "You've been poisoned, and I'm letting this stupid mating lust and my stupid emotions get in the way."

"Ava," his tone turned deadly serious, "come back to me now."

I balked a bit at that, but when he looked at me with those pleading blue eyes, I couldn't resist. Carefully, I stretched over him once more. But this time I kept my mouth firmly out of kissing range.

"Listen closely." He tried again to reach for me. This time he succeeded in wrapping one arm around my lower back. "You are many things: beautiful, smart," his warm smile turned my insides to jelly, "fiesty."

"Hey," I warned playfully. He wasn't free of danger, but hearing him talk settled my nerves.

"You are all these things. But stupid?" His expression changed. He was the serious Rhonar warrior now. "That is not a quality you possess. The mating lust between us is a sacred sign that we are made for each other." His words grew solemn. "And your feelings? They are not stupid. I was in the void where no such emotion traveled for so long. I lost hope to ever feel again." His gaze captured mine. "Yet you gave that to me. Hope, laughter, joy, even the worry for you, the fear that you'll be hurt, the despair that you could leave me —it is all worth it to feel what I do for you."

I didn't move, didn't breathe. Time ticked by between us. I had to hear it aloud. "And what *do* you feel?"

"I—"

The door creaked open, and Brok and Jadara strode inside. I screeched, jumping off Xelan and hiking up the front of my cat-suit.

Jadara snickered. "Were we interrupting?"

"Ye—No!" I waved my hands in front of me, my cheeks heating horribly. "I was just trying to keep him warm."

"I see." She hiked up a bright red brow.

Brok closed the door behind them, then held up a metal cup. "The antidote is ready, according to our rebel friend." He eyed the alien woman with doubt.

"I told you, it is." Snorting she took the cup from him and gave it to me. "He's absolutely paranoid. But really, this is the antidote, I swear it."

"Thank you." Somehow I believed her. I knelt by Xelan's side and held the cup to his lips. If she were lying, I'd think my mate would know, even in his weakened state. "Ready?"

"Yes." He gulped down the liquid, closing his eyes as he did so.

When he finished the contents, I put it to the side and watched his chest rise and fall.

"Now, what?" Brok asked from his standing position by the door. He always seemed to be the constant guardian. I saw now why Xelan had posed as the Elite and Brok as his bodyguard. I'd never met someone more stoic.

I thought all this as a distraction, both for the time it would take the antidote to do its job, and from thinking about Xelan's words before we were interrupted.

It didn't help.

"Now," Jedara rose to stand on the opposite side of the door, "we wait."

I inwardly groaned. Time with nothing to do but think. *Perfect.*

Chapter 16

XELAN

I'D BEEN A DRAV FOOL. ALLOWING MERCY TOWARD THAT dishonorable Craxion bastard? *Crex!* I thought as I laid on the pallet, waiting for the antidote to have an effect. I'd let myself be poisoned in the middle of a battle. I was seething and yet, suffering from embarrassment, another unwelcome feeling.

What I'd said to Ava was true. Having these negative emotions was worth it to be able to feel for her. It was a blessing from Celestia, and I would not take it for granted. But my battle tactics would need adjusting to be able to fight with emotions swirling inside me. For so long I'd sensed the feelings of others, using them to read my enemy. Now I had my own. Yet I understood so little of them.

Except my feelings for my Truxoria. My beautiful mate was a gift beyond imagining, and if she'd let me, I'd worship and cherish her for the rest of our lives.

The mating lust rose steadily as my body healed. The effects of the poison waned. I needed to complete the bond, if Ava consented. Until it was claimed, the desire would continue to rise until we were both driven mad with it. Although, as I stared at Brok's grim face, Ava's worried brow, and the neutral expression from our new ally, I almost laughed aloud. There could not be a worse setting for sealing a mate bond.

It was time to leave.

Rising from the pallet, two sets of hands tended me instantly. Ava's warm palms on my chest made my kedara run hot. Brok at my back kept me steady. "I'm all right." I grabbed her hands in mine for a beat to reassure her. "I'm well."

Her adorable little nose wrinkled. "I don't think it's been enough time." She turned to the blue-skinned female. "What do you think?"

The female shrugged. "I don't know his chemistry. But if he can get up that quickly, I'd say he'll be fine."

"See?" I smiled at Ava. Inclining my head toward the female, whose name I still didn't know, I added, "Thank you..."

"Jadara," she filled in and gave a two-fingered greeting. "Undercover rebel at your service."

My pulse quickened. Our new ally was a rebel? If that was true, our mission had taken a positive turn. Brok passed me my armor. As I positioned it over my chest and strapped in, I checked the interior lining. The flash key, letters, and seal met my fingers. I palmed them in my fists.

"She seems to be telling the truth," Brok offered begrudgingly. "I questioned her while she brewed your antidote."

"Which worked as I said, didn't it?" Her smug grin was aimed at my brather.

He grunted his assent.

"If you can lead us to the other rebels," I said, claiming her attention again, "I'll give you these." I held up the evidence for her to see.

Jadara squinted, her bright red brows drawing inward. "What's on that?" She motioned to the flash key.

Ava tucked into my side, wrapping an arm around my waist. Pointing to my hand, she said, "It's part of the evidence I told you about."

Sensing no ill intentions from her, and since the female had saved my life with her antidote, I presented it to her. "It has a collection of holo-vids and docs showing all of Denthar Calth's dealings. Everything you can imagine, and some you probably can't." My stomach soured as I recalled those files. "And he's not the only member of the Craxion Elite on there."

"You're serious?" Taking the flash key from me, she turned it to the light at the center of the room.

"Yes." I presented the rest to our rebel ally. "These letters and seal solidify the proof." I put my free arm around Ava's shoulders. "We collected it together."

Flicking her gaze from me then to my mate and back, Jadara asked in whispered awe, "How?"

"The bastard set a trap for us in his study." I squeezed my Truxoria a bit closer to my side. "Used that evidence as bait to lure us in and challenge me to that match."

She snorted. "Didn't work out too well for him."

"No." I felt no remorse at Calth's death. "It didn't."

"Well, if this is everything you say, then you've done what I couldn't do for too many cycles under his eye." The bitterness in her voice matched the feelings of hate wafting from her. "And all that I had to go through."

"I'm so sorry for what you suffered." Ava stepped out from under my arm and toward the female. "I had something similar happen to me."

Jadara cocked her head to the side. "You were whipped?"

My mate nodded, and her pain over the memory seeped under my skin. I matched her stride and held her once more.

"Then you understand." Jadara pointed to the bandages covering her. "But don't worry. I'm a quick healer and good with medicines." She winked at Ava. "It's worth it for this." Tugging the evidence into a belt at her waist, she acknowledged us each in turn. "Thank you, all of you."

Brok and I put our fists to our sternums, between our double hearts, and bowed. Jadara was a courageous female to go undercover as a slave for the rebellion. Her emotions showed no deception, and I believed that what she said was true.

"We will accompany you safely from here and to your fellow allies." I would need to wait a beat longer to claim my mate. Our mission was almost complete. We needed this one spark to light the fire. "When your numbers have been secured, we will leave."

"You won't fight with us?" Her eyes shifted between Brok and me, likely taking in our size and armor.

"It's not our way," I said carefully. In truth, we had fought in alien conflicts before. But this was an internal Craxion matter. If not for the Elite's engaging in interplanetary slavery—morally repugnant and illegal even in the Meta Sector—we likely wouldn't be involved at all. We wanted to stir the rebels to fight for themselves, not fight for them. "If you're to overcome the corruption of the Elites and attain your freedom, you'll need to do so by your own hands."

Her answering smirk was full of pluck. "So be it."

*

THE REBELS WERE FURTHER ALONG THAN WE'D THOUGHT. A physical underground network wound between different homes all throughout the city. They had dug tunnels with dead ends and false entrances to throw outsiders off the trail. Code words and secret phrases provided an extra layer of protection. Their people were trained, organized, and prepared.

And their numbers were growing.

As their leaders rifled through the letters and reviewed the holo-files, their faces remained impassive. But after the final holo-vid clicked to a close, the head of their trio stepped forward and bowed low. "Thank you." His eyes glowed bright as he rose. "This is what we've been waiting for."

Spans later, with Brok and I pitching in ideas, the rebels had a full assault plan ready. When Craxon's suns rose on the horizon, it would mark the beginning of the end. Their forces were ready, and the evidence we'd brought would convince the holdouts as we planned.

As we made to leave them, the leader who had thanked us earlier, bade us farewell with a warning. "A red day will dawn."

I hoped he was right. But I needed to get my mate and my companions off this planet before the true battle began. "May Celestia guide you to victory." I gripped his forearm in the customary Rhonar acknowledgment of another warrior, and then took my mate's hand as we turned to go.

Jadara guided us back through the tunnels so we could retrieve the catars. "When this is all over," she grasped Ava's free hand and grinned, "I'm going on a space cruise! After that, I want to see you again. Would you visit me?"

Ava returned the smile. "Yes, I'd like that."

"It's a promise, then." Opening the hatch that led to a patchy dirt trail in the middle of Calth's property, she ushered us through. "Until the stars align, and we meet again."

"Be safe and take care!" Ava waved her hand in what I guessed was a Terran farewell gesture.

"Thank you, again, Jadara." I saluted her once more, my fist upon my sternum. "I'm in your debt."

"Nah, we're good." She laughed. "You lit the fire we needed. I'm satisfied with that."

Brok nodded at her, and she closed the hatch behind us.

"Well that was something." Ava motioned to the hatch and then the mansion in the distance. "I think I've had enough adventure to last a while."

"I hope…" Glancing over my shoulder at my brather, I silently willed him to leave. What I needed to say was for my mate alone.

Brok caught my eye. "I'll go and fetch the catars. You both wait here."

Neither of us said anything after he left, although I desired to tell her everything. We stared at each other under the planet's bright starlight. My hearts pounded hard. I wanted so much to sweep her in my arms and never let her go. But, did she want to stay with me? She'd been through so much—stolen from her people, ripped from her life. What if what I had to offer wasn't enough? What if I'd fail her? *I've failed before.*

An unbidden memory of my saester surfaced as I stood there. Calzara's soft tawny eyes, so like our maether's had been, formed in my mind. Her final words to me as the virus took hold of her ripped through me. "Don't stop trying to find your mate." Her hand gripping mine, and her breath hitching, haunted me. "You deserve to feel again."

I don't. She was wrong.

I'd failed to protect her, my saester, the female who raised me after our parents died in an accident. She had given me everything. Not much older than me, she'd dedicated her life to helping me into malehood. After our enemy released the biological weapon that targeted our females, she hung on longer than anyone…for me. But in the end, I couldn't save her.

What did I have to offer a mate, if I couldn't even protect my saester?

"Xelan?" Ava's soft voice brought me back. "Your sister? Is that who you're talking about?"

Celestia, had I said that aloud? "Yes," I said, not wanting to hide it. Having already been in the hunger phase when she died, my own body eating through my emotions like a starving male, I never experienced the grief over her loss. It hit me now as hard as Rhonar steel. "I lost her to the enemy, to the virus they unleashed."

Ava stepped closer to me, her hands sliding around my hips. "I'm so sorry."

"My parents had died many orbits before that." A lump lodged in my throat. "She raised me."

The sorrow that my mate felt on my behalf mixed with my own. Yet somehow it brought me comfort. My Truxoria's emotions, even her sadness, wrapped around me and bathed me in warmth. "You're not alone anymore. I'm here."

And she was. So much so that I could feel my hearts beat for her, my body harden for her, my soul align with hers. She was so much a part of me already. If I claimed her, how much closer would we become? I wanted to know. Maybe, I didn't deserve a mate. Maybe, I had failed to protect Calzara. But it had been my saester's final wish. Even as she left this world, she thought of me. Now, the universe had granted me Ava.

I wasn't fool enough to deny fate, even if grief and regret warred within me.

"Thank you, Ava." I pulled her closer, breathing in her floral scent. "I'm unworthy."

"You?" She looked up at me, surprise clear in her face and her emotions.

"Yes, I—" I choked on the words. How did I admit my deepest shame to my mate? I sighed. She deserved to know. "I promised to find her a cure. I searched the galaxies, hunted down every lead." My memories of those awful days overwhelmed me for a beat. "But I never found one."

"That's not your fault," she shouted at me, her tiny hands fisting on my chest.

"You don't understand." I held her hands against my armor. "I made her a vow, and she fought the virus for too long because of it. She suffered because she believed in me. And I failed her."

"No." Her hair flew behind her as she shook her head vehemently. "She fought because she loved you. I didn't know her, but I'd bet she was a fighter, right? She wouldn't just quit, not if there was a way to live."

My grief lifted a bit at that. Calzara *had* been a fighter as much as any Rhonar warrior I'd ever known. She was high-spirited and courageous. Just like my Terran mate. "Yes, she was."

"Then, she never expected you to save her. She fought because that's who she was." Her bottom lip swelled as she bit down on it. Her emotions hit me—she was holding something back.

"What is it?" I gripped her shoulder lightly. "Truxoria, what are you not saying?"

"I, well, it's not my place to say." She tugged at her hair, a gesture that belied her nerves.

"You are my mate, Ava. You are the other half of my soul." I hugged her in a tight grip before releasing her so she could continue. "There is nothing you cannot say to me."

"It's just that…" She sighed as if working up to it. "If you want to honor her memory, then you should respect who she was. Your guilt weakens her strength." Her arms wrapped around my waist again. "Celebrate that strength. Maybe she didn't win, but she fought, and that deserves to be remembered as a part of her story."

Stunned. I was utterly stunned. No one had rendered me as speechless as the female in my arms. I had never framed the loss in such a manner. My battle to save my saester, my perceived failure, weakened her story?

Yes, I could see that.

Calzara was a fighter. She was strong. Had I never vowed to find a cure, she still would have fought. It was who *she* was, who she had always been. I needed to honor her death as she had been in life.

Staring in awe at my mate, I said, "You're right."

"I know." Her low chuckle rippled through me, washing away the grief and firing my blood. Her answering scent of desire perfumed the air. "Xelan?" she whispered, an undercurrent of desire clear in her tone. "Take me away from this."

That I could do.

Chapter 17

AVA

XELAN WANTED NOTHING MORE THAN TO GET US ALL OFF the planet, but more than half the night was spent, and the Rhonar ship would not be back in orbit until midday tomorrow. So we returned to their house on Craxon, riding the catars at breakneck speed. Maena met us at the front door, her lavender hands flapping a greeting. Tallis stood behind her, smiling indulgently at his wife. She insisted on checking us over before she would declare us fit and send us to bed.

I stood now in the bathroom of the room I'd been given before, staring at the 3-D projection the reflector produced of me. Except for some minor bruises, tousled hair, and red eyes, I was mostly okay. I laughed. Well, as okay as I could get anyway. Stepping into the strange black shower, I mentally prepared for the glittery gel cleaning substance that was way too slime-like. I wanted to be clean more than I cared about how.

It still sucked.

"Ugh, haven't these aliens heard of water?" I shivered as the foam hit me, wiping away all remnants of the gel-slime. It left me clean and dry…and without any other reason to stall. Yes, I was stalling. My alien warrior with the body and strength of an ancient deity, not to mention the prowess of a sex god, and a gentle side he showed only to me, stood outside the door. So maybe I was having a wee bit of human insecurity issues.

I mean does he have to be that perfect. I sighed, staring at the next projection of me. My hair ran straight down my back without a hint of wave or shape. Hips wider than I'd like rounded to a stomach that was bigger than I wanted. My nose was small and my lips were thin. And…

"And this is stupid."

I waved the projection away. Xelan's desire for me was palpable, and maybe it was mating lust, but the way he looked at me was like nothing else. He stared at me as if I were a person to be treasured, the center of his universe. I wasn't going to pick at my insecurities. I'd worked too damn hard to fall for that mind trap. I was an amazing person, and I deserved love, passion, and everything that this alien warrior offered me. All I had to do was be brave enough to claim it.

I opened the door, wearing nothing.

Xelan stood with his chest bare in only a pair of soft sleep pants that rode low on his hips. He growled and held out his hand to me. "Truxoria."

I took it and went into the shelter of his arms. His skin was so warm, and his rich chocolate and spice scent surrounded me.

"Ava," he said my name with reverence. I shivered in his embrace. The kiss he gave me was soft, exploratory, like he wanted to lure me in. I melted under his gentle ministrations. When he pulled back, my lips—and other parts of me—throbbed.

"Don't stop." I didn't care what he did or how he did it. As my desire rose, I only wanted more of everything.

"I need you, my mate." He placed my hands against his chest. "Feel my hearts beat for you."

I did, strong and sure they beat beneath my palms, both of them. *Two hearts,* I thought, smiling inwardly as the rhythm quickened. *And all mine.*

His dark chocolate scent surrounded me, making my body heat, but his words touched my spirit.

"I thought I understood emotions, despite not having any. I was a fool." He held my waist, pulling me flush with his body. "Everything I feel for you makes my life before you a pale shadow. You are my sun."

"Oh Xelan." Emotions clogged my throat. I'd never had anyone care for me so deeply. "I thought I'd always known what I wanted, who I was, and who I wanted to be." My heart pounded so hard, but it beat in rhythm with his two. In his arms, I discovered something more, something deeper, a love that I never even dreamed of.

"I've fought for everything I've ever had. But I don't want to fight anymore, and I don't want to be free." I kissed the middle of his chest between my hands. "I want to be yours."

His answer was to crush his mouth to mine. There was no gentleness this time, but I wanted none. Nothing laid between us any longer. We'd bared our souls to each other, and all that was left was to make them one.

I hooked my leg around his waist as he guided me to the bed. The sheet felt silky beneath my skin. My pussy was wet and my clit was aching. I reached for him to drag him to me, but he was not to be deterred.

"I will not rush this. We are bonding more than our bodies," he said brushing his fingertips slowly along my calf, my knee, and the inside of my thigh. "This is the beginning of our lives as true mates." His blue eyes sparkled wickedly in the firelight. "And I will take my time enjoying every part of you."

I moaned. My desire was already at a fever pitch. How long could I last against this exquisite torment? When his fingers grazed my ribs and the underside of my breasts, I nearly jumped off the bed.

"So sensitive." His gruff tone fired my blood. "So mine."

"Please, Xelan," I begged. I had no shame left. I needed him, my alien mate.

"Soon." He stretched out beside me, taking my right nipple into his mouth and sucking hard.

I bucked into his touch. "More."

With his hands free, he used one to squeeze the breast that he licked and sucked while pinching and caressing the nipple of the other. The throbbing in my pussy drove me wild, and I inched my hand down my body. He released my breast with a loud pop, before diving on the other. I moaned as my fingers grazed my clit. But he let go of my breast to grab hold of my wrist.

"That's my pleasure." His eyes held mine transfixed. "Let me."

He slid down my body, wasting no time in using that long, talented tongue. When it began to vibrate against my aching clit, he plunged two thick fingers inside me. I went off like a rocket. It was a hard, fast orgasm that sent me straight into orbit. I floated somewhere above my body with no desire to return to it.

As he continued to lap and suck at me, I came crashing into myself. My nerves went on high alert as lust gripped me again. I had never been a multi-orgasmic person. Not alone, and definitely, not with former partners. But, here I was, ready for more after barely coming off my first peak.

I stared down at him, hardly believing this alien was mine. "Xelan," I said, truly unable to wait any longer. "Claim me. Fuck me. Make me yours."

As if sensing my need, he rose above me. "You're ready, my Truxoria?"

"So ready." I tugged at the waistband of his pants. "Off."

He chuckled. "As you wish."

Oh I wished all right. He stood and slid the loose pants down his trim hips and thick thighs. I nearly drooled when his massive cock sprang free—and maybe, held my breath. *How the hell is it going to fit?* He was enormous, like forget horse-hung, this was…I didn't even have a comparison.

And what was…?

"Let me feel you." I waved for him to come closer. "I want to touch."

His growl did things to my insides. But I was too in shock over his equipment. It was human-looking enough, besides its size, but it had something extra at the base. I fingered the appendage gently. It looked a bit like a smaller cock. It was knob-shaped and bulbous at the top and thinner at the base. "What is this?"

"Do human males not possess a crux?" He raised one brow.

"No." I wrapped my hand around his cock, marveling that I couldn't close my fingers all the way around. Then, I dragged them down his length. "What's it for?"

"Crex," he groaned. "That feels good."

"I'm glad." I laughed, enjoying this brief control over my big warrior. "But not crex. We were talking about your crux. What does it do?"

"You'll see." He stilled my hand and brought it above my head on the bed. Claiming my free hand, he brought that one to follow the first and wrapped the sheet around them both. "Don't move your hands."

"I won't," I spread my knees wide, "if you show me what that crux is for."

Hooking my legs over his elbows, he pulled me to the foot of the bed. The sheet tightened deliciously around my bound hands. As he remained standing, my body was laid out for him like a feast.

"Perfect," he said, starting down at me.

My cheeks flushed. I squirmed, feeling my wetness slide along my inner thighs. Before I could complain at his making me wait, he lodged his cock at my entrance. A little slice of trepidation went through me at the thought of all that fitting inside me, but excitement won over. "Do it."

But my alien was not to be commanded. "Slowly," he said in a husky voice. "You're wet enough to take me, but you're not to feel pain."

My laughter came out as a snort. Only my alien could demand such things. A fraction a time, he pushed inside me. My pussy clenched at his invasion. I stretched around him, the most amazing sensation. And…it didn't hurt. It felt fucking incredible. I urged him on with my heels against his ass. When he at last bottomed out inside me, we both groaned.

"You feel so crexing tight, so perfect." His pinched expression showed how much he was holding back.

I didn't want that. I wanted all of him. "Xelan, you don't have to worry. You won't break me. I want you, all of you."

He smirked. "Oh you'll get all." That's when that knob, his crux, which rested against my clit, started to vibrate.

And so did his cock.

"No fucking way!" I screamed as my entire body lit up like a damn forest fire.

He didn't answer, instead he took my hips in his big hands, pulled all the way out, and slammed home. And then he did it again, and again.

"Ah," I cried, my sensitive pussy pulsing in time to his thrusts. His vibrating cock and crux hit every nerve, some I had no idea I even had.

The orgasm built inside me like a tidal wave, ready to sweep me away. I wanted that, reached for it.

"Come for me, Ava." He leaned over me and removed the sheet from my hands. Then, he dragged me upright, so his cock hit me impossibly deeper. "Come now."

The new angle hit a spot inside me that had my toes curling and my mind spinning. "Yes!"

As my desire spiked and the orgasm hit, he thrust faster. The vibrations increased, and I exploded in a million pieces. He roared his satisfaction. White hot heat filled me as he emptied himself inside me.

My love, I heard his voice in my head. *Now, you're truly mine.*

"What the?" I shook my head, his still hard cock pulsing inside me. It was a gentle wave now, unlike the vibrations of earlier and it felt so good after our shared orgasm. "Was that you?"

"Yes," he said aloud. *We're joined. It is the mating mind speak.*

What? I thought at him. *Why didn't you tell me?*

Bad surprise?

I considered it. Having another person in my head should make me super uncomfortable. But this? This didn't. It felt right, like it was supposed to be this way. *No, I don't think it is.*

"Good," he said aloud and kissed my nose. "Don't worry. I can't read your mind or anything like that. It's just want you want me to hear."

"Well, some boundaries *are* healthy." I squeezed his cock with my inner walls. "But I like being close to you."

"I enjoy it too, my Truxoria." He began to vibrate a bit more rapidly inside me.

My eyes widened as the pulsing stirred my desire again. "How are you not soft?"

"After one time?" He cocked his head to the side. "Human males soften so quickly?"

I wriggled against that seeking crux at my clit. "Forget that. Just do it again."

"With pleasure, my mate." His thrusts began all over again, and I basked in our connection. "With pleasure."

Chapter 18

XELAN

THE NIGHT PASSED IN A STATE OF ECSTASY. MY MATE, MY Truxoria, was mine, and I hers. The soul deep bond radiated inside me. I held her close after the mating lust sated for a time. When her breathing evened and her body relaxed on top of mine, I allowed my eyes to close. Yet the memory of her cries as I'd brought her to the peak over and over were still ringing in my ears. It was with that incredible melody that I succumbed to sleep.

When the orange light filtered in the room the next day, it was closer to mid-afternoon. Ava still lay atop me, gently snoring. I hated to wake her, but it was time to leave this place and start our true life together. "Ava," I said softy, shaking her with care. "Wake up."

She grumbled. Her hair was in complete disarray around her head, and her sleepy eyes blinked up at me. She was beautiful. The half grin she gave me shot straight to my cock. I groaned. As much as I wanted to claim her again, if I did so now, we'd never leave.

"Morning," she said, swiping at her eyes. "What time is it?"

I hugged her tighter. "Based on the light coming in, I'd say after lunch."

"Hmm," she hummed and a full smile lit up her face. "Guess you wore me out."

"As much as I'd love to do so again," I shifted to roll her onto her side, "it's time for us to go."

"Go?" She jumped up, kicking the sheet off her as she did. "Like go, go? Like off this planet, go?"

I chuckled at her enthusiasm. In truth, I was as eager to leave. "Yes."

"Woohoo!" She pumped her fist in the air. "I am so ready for that."

I rose from the bed, stretching my back as I did so. My Rhonar brathers would be in orbit by now. We'd have to make the trek to the ship, but after that, we'd be free, our mission complete.

I caught her staring at me as I contemplated our departure. "What is it?"

Her mouth fell open, and she pointed. "Xelan, your arms."

"What?" I held my hands up to examine them. What I found sent heat radiating through my chest. "It's for you." My katra glowed red as my kedara moved through it, expanding over my wrists. The delicate pattern crossed in a floral array with wing shapes at the center. "These markings on my arms are a part of us, but it's formed from a special metal."

From the expression on her face, I could practically see the wheels in her inquisitive brain turning. *How?* her mental voice asked. I wasn't sure if she meant to mind speak, but I grinned at her doing it nonetheless.

"When a male reaches the age of maturity, we heat the metal and pour it over his arms."

"Ouch!" she winced.

"It doesn't hurt. It's warmed enough to be liquid, but it doesn't burn like other materials." I waved it off. "Anyway, we use our kedara, that's the energy inside of us, to manipulate it into shape."

"That's incredible." She touched the markings on my arms reverently.

"My shoulders are for those males who are of my *Brather*. It's a special vow we make to a selected few from among all our brathers." I held her free hand in mine. "Brok is of my *Brather*."

"That doesn't surprise me." She kissed my shoulder, then pointed to my bicep. "And these?"

"Those represent my family. The star shape is my saester."

Another kiss to my arm, then she licked a path downward.

I sucked in a breath as lust rose in me again. It should have been sated now that we were bonded, but it seemed I would always desire my mate.

The answering scent of her arousal reached my nose. She straightened. "What about your forearms?"

"They signify our special gift. My empathic ability in my case." Crex her scent was driving me wild.

"And now, you have these." She circled the new marks on my wrist lightly. "They're beautiful. But how?"

"When we bond to our mates, the katra expands." I stared at the markings, loving how perfectly they matched her. "And it forms to signify our Truxoria. This is how I see you." It was a subconscious process, but it was how I saw Ava in my heart. "Wings because although you belong to me, you are always free. I will never hold you back." I brushed my fingers under her eyes as tears formed there. "And opening flower petals as I want to see you bloom into the fullness of who you are, and whoever you want to be." I chuckled and sniffed her hair. "Plus your scent is the same as a Yalian flower."

My scent? Her mental voice squawked the question.

I growled. *Yes. Your scent.*

Oh.

It was all the answer I needed to claim my mate all over again.

AVA

We didn't leave Craxon until early evening. After emerging from the room, we showed Brok, Maena, and Tallis the new katra on Xelan's arms and declared our mate-bond complete. They all cheered, although I imagined they'd already suspected as much, since we hadn't left the room for…well, awhile.

Even when Maena left us food at the door, we'd hardly stopped to eat. Brok, who I knew was caught in the Rhonar void, managed to smile when we told them the news. But it didn't reach his eyes, and although, our mate-bond meant hope for all Rhonar, he couldn't feel that hope.

It gutted me.

What about the florins, you told me about. I mind spoke to Xelan. Admittedly, I wasn't sure at first about this whole telepathy thing, but it was more like mentally talking than mind-reading. I couldn't tell what my mate was thinking unless he "spoke" to me and vice versa.

They can help temporarily, but it's not a permanent fix. His arms held me as we sat atop the catar on our way to his ship.

"I know, but if what you've said turns out to be the truth, then he, and the other Rhonar too, deserve to feel hopeful." I sighed. *Even if it's just for a moment.*

"You're right, my Truxoria." His chest was against my back, and even through his armor, he emitted warmth.

Xelan believed that humans, Terrans, as he called my people, were descendants of the Rhonar. Long ago, his kind had ventured into space to settle colonies on other planets. "Do you really think Earth could be a lost colony?"

"I do." He kissed the top of my head and urged the catar into a faster pace.

The fact that Xelan and I bonded meant that other humans might be able to bond with his brathers. And if that were true, then his species would be saved from extinction and his brathers from a life of emptiness. I could feel his anxiety to reach the ship grow with each passing second.

In truth, I felt the same. Not just because I wanted off this planet, but I needed to study this mate-bond. I was a scientist after all, and this would be the perfect opportunity to put my skills to work. I wanted to help the Rhonar, and there was still my people to save. I had to know what happened to the rest of the crew, after we were attacked. I sagged in his arms. "There's so much to do."

He held me up, brushing his nose through my hair. "One piece at a time, my mate."

My sensible alien. *Yes. Can't build a Roman city—or a space station—overnight.*

I tried to relax after that and enjoy the ride to the ship. Truly, I did. But catar travel would never be my favorite mode of transportation. When we reached the spot where the Rhonar spacecraft sat in orbit some time later, I nearly jumped off the six-legged creature.

"Whoa," Xelan said as he caught me before I could hop down. "I don't know whose more excited to be leaving, you, me, or them." He thumbed at Maena and Tallis. The Kinisian couple, as I'd learned their species, would be traveling with us until we could get them transport home or take them there. They bounced with anticipation.

"It's probably still me." I kissed the spot between his hearts. I was a bit nervous to live with a whole group of aliens, but Xelan assured me that we'd have our own quarters and privacy to explore our bond. I looked forward to the journey.

As we transported to the ship, my jaw dropped. The Rhonar craft was like something out of a sci-fi dream. Equipped for battle, it had all the features you'd expect on a fighting vessel from laser blasters to a reinforced hull to a tactical bridge. Yet it was also created for deep space travel, and so, it had amazing creature comforts like a gym, ample quarters, a dining hall, a lounge, and even a holo-room that the crew used for strategy meetings and recreation alike.

"This is incredible!" I whirled in circles everywhere we went to take it all in.

Xelan laughed. "I'm glad you approve."

When the tour was complete, we headed toward the briefing room. Xelan and Brok were to give a report on the mission, and Xelan and I were going to reveal our mate-bond to the senior staff. I gulped when we entered, but Maena and Tallis were also invited to attend as witnesses and to give their account, which made me feel a bit better.

Seated around an oval table sat a solemn contingent of Rhonar warriors.

I sighed. It was more painful than I imagined to see these males as emotionless as robots. They deserved more, and with luck, my people could give it to them.

After the briefing, Xelan pulled me into his lap. "Florin!" he shouted as we had agreed earlier.

If we were going to give hope to his brathers, then I wanted them to feel it, and with luck, they'd carry the memory of that feeling with them.

A blue creature appeared in the center of the table with a pop. My head jerked back and almost smacked Xelan in the face. *Sorry,* I muttered in our mind speak. I was just so surprised. Whatever I expected from my mate's description of the telepathic, inter-dimensional traveling aliens, this wasn't it. The florin was like a cross between a corgi, a hamster, and a fox all mixed together. As I stared at its white belly, blue fur, and three bushy tails, I scrunched my nose. The creature was utterly foreign, and yet, I recognized it.

Have I seen this florin before? I twisted my head this way and that as if I could somehow put the pieces together.

Xelan gave my middle a squeeze. *When we were rescued you from the slave market, we had to keep you calm.* He cocked his chin toward the florin. *They were the same one who helped.*

I didn't know what to make of this development, but I decided to think on it later. *Can you ask it to help the Rhonar now?*

"Yes, I will," he said aloud. "Florin, project hope."

The gathered Rhonar had been silently observing this interplay, but one with several silver pieces on his chest armor balked. "What is this warrior?"

Xelan bowed his head at the male. "Forgive me, Commander, but we have news to share, and it was requested by Ava here." He placed one hand at my shoulder.

"The Terran female?" another male asked. He had purple eyes that made his expression appear more animated than the rest.

"Yes." As Xelan spoke, the florin emanated a cooing sound. The atmosphere in the room shifted as did the Rhonar in their seats. "My brathers," he cried passionately, "Celestia has granted us a gift beyond compare. Ava of Earth is my mate." He rose, setting me to my feet as he did so. Linking our hands together, he held our arms high and showed the symbols on his wrists. "Behold, my Truxoria."

Xelan kissed me then, a show of passion that left no doubt to his feelings. *You are my everything, Ava. We are One. Never doubt that I love you.*

Tears filled my eyes as he continued the kiss. *I love you too,* I whispered in our special mind speak.

The answering shouts of joy, the gasps of surprise, and even the barrage of questions would be a sound I'd cherish in my memories for the rest of my days. At last, the Rhonar had hope. Together we would find my missing crew-mates, travel to Earth, forge an alliance, and bring peace to these alien warriors. I believed that with every fiber of my being.

What would happen first? Well, only the stars knew.

But with the alien warrior I loved by my side, anything was possible.

Epilogue
BROK

THE PARTY LASTED THREE DAYS. FLORIN AFTER FLORIN popped to our dimension to pump emotions into my brathers as we celebrated this iconic mate-bond between our species. I indulged in the chance to feel. But it was fleeting. Until we found our mates, we would suffer. And my time was close, too close. If I failed my internal struggle, if the void took me, I'd become…

"Never." I wouldn't allow myself to even think of the alternative. *Death first*, I thought darkly.

I banged the desk attached to the wall in my quarters. The sensation of my fist hitting the metal was a mild balm to my soul.

I hadn't felt, truly felt in so long. The florins' projected emotions were like a distant star. I could see the light twinkling far off, but I'd never feel its warmth. I yearned for the heat. Seeing Xelan with the brave little Terran stoked the dying embers of my spirit. Ava was a star that shone brighter than any I'd seen before, a hope to us all.

How long would I remain in shadow?

My brothers laughed from time to time, even if they didn't experience true mirth. They were able to replicate the appearance of emotion so that at least it looked real to an outsider. Perhaps, they did it to convince themselves as well.

I could not.

I didn't have it in me to express that which I didn't feel. And so, I was deemed a statue, the stoic one of the Rhonar warriors. I was the rock that would not bend, the stone that would not break.

But I was breaking. The cracks formed inside me, letting the void take hold.

I pulled out the stool that rested under the desk and threw a leg over it. With my elbows resting on the smooth surface, I contemplated my next move.

The spacecraft we inhabited was a deep space vessel, equipped for battle and exploration alike. Currently, our mission was in the Meta Sector. Discovering the fate of the missing Terran crew was added to that list of orders.

As was my mission.

"Find Earth." Commander Torian had tasked five of my brothers, including me, to spread out and track down any leads.

I opened the holo-pad that sat on a stand in the center of the desk. Flipping it to a map of the Gaian Sector, I studied the strange star patterns. From the intel we'd gathered, we knew Earth resided in this less populated area of the universe. As a remote and distant planet, it made sense as to why there was so little information about it. The sole reason we knew anything at all was that space pirates had kidnapped Terrans from it thousands of orbits ago, and the descendants of those abducted had left clues.

Now, with Ava filling in the blank spots, we had a real chance of discovering its location.

"I'll be the one." I didn't doubt my brathers' skills. Each warrior was intelligent and capable of the mission, but I had more reason than anyone.

I stared at the map, willing it to give me the answers I sought. "Celestia, be my guide." I hadn't prayed to our goddess since I was a youngling. I didn't think she cared for me at all, but I had nothing left to lose. If there was even a chance she'd help me, I had to try. Time was running thin for me.

I needed to find my mate, to bond her, to claim her.

Before the void claimed me.

Thank you for reading! Did you enjoy? Please add your review because nothing helps an author more and encourages readers to take a chance on a book than a review.

Want a special **BONUS SCENE** with Ava and Xelan utilizing the ship's holo-room as they explore their new mate bond? Then join my newsletter HERE for that upcoming bonus release, and all the latest sales, reveals, and giveaways!

And don't miss more in the Earth Brides & Alien Warriors series with book two, ALIEN'S MATE, available now! Find out what happens to Brok. Turn the page for a sneak peek!

This book has been edited and proofed. However, pesky grammar gremlins are like space dust, you just can't get rid of it! If you would like to help fight the battle against them, however, please feel free to send them to AlienBookLover@gmail.com with the Subject Line: GRAMMAR GREMLINS.

Thank you and happy reading!

Sneak Peek of Alien's Mate
SAGE

"If you don't turn on right this second, I'm sending you to the scrap pile." I huffed at the blasted fuel converter. "See how you like being space dust." Clasping the astro-wrench in my fist, I beat it against the machine's outer hull. "I'm warning you." A clip-clip sound was the only response to my threat. "Okay, on three. One…" Another strike from my tool. "Two…" Cranking gears groaned in answer.

"What happens on three?"

The voice startled me from my rantings. I jerked up, knocking my head on the top of the fuel converter. "What the—?"

"Oy sorry." A gentle hand landed on my shoulder and guided me from the infernal machine. "You all right now?"

"Oh, Dr. Harper." I rose from a crouch and wiped stray fuel droplets from my coveralls. "What are you doing here?"

"Apologies for disturbing you while you're working, Lieutenant Kadaran." The good doctor ran a hand through her curly hair. The tight coils sprang forward, framing the doctor's high cheekbones and thoughtful eyes. Her long white lab coat, while not the most flattering, did not derail from her statuesque form.

I sighed, feeling like a goblin in comparison. The fluorescent lights overhead would make me appear ghost-like, but with the doctor's perfectly smooth brown complexion, she was highlighted like a goddess. "Just Sage is fine. No formalities needed." I bit my lip and stamped down the jealousy that bubbled inside me. It wasn't the doctor's fault that I struggled with some insecurities. Having three gorgeous sisters would do that to a girl. "And it's not a worry. How can I help you, Dr. Harper?"

"Please call me, Grace." She smiled with straight white teeth. "Well, I'm afraid I have to remind you about your check-up."

"Now?" I all but whined. The only thing worse than dealing with the moonbase's decrepit machinery was a medical visit.

"Well," the doctor looked around the corridor as if confirming we were alone, "it's been a week since your inoculations and implant. So, I'd like to test that everything is working as it should."

I laughed aloud. "Doc, I'm in no danger of pregnancy. Trust me." Circling the birth control implant under my forearm, I patted it in reassurance. "And I don't feel sick or any side effects from the shots." My grin was lopsided. "Think I'm good."

"Oh but—"

Before the doctor could continue, Taylor, computer genius and best friend extraordinaire, popped into view from the far corner and jogged up to us. Her palms went to her knees as she sucked in several breaths. "I-I…" She struggled to get in air.

"Whoa there, Tay." I patted her back lightly. "You okay?"

"May I help you?" The doctor—no wait, she'd said to think of her as Grace—took out a mini-scanner and ran it over Taylor from head to toe.

Whoosh. The air squeezed out of her. "That was a run." Taylor dusted off her jeans and rose to her full height, coming in several inches below Grace, and yet still a finger's length taller than me. "I'm good, Doctor, thanks." Waving the scanner away and bouncing in her sneakers, she turned her attention on me. "Sage, you won't believe it, but the com signal has gone out on the satellite station again." Her devilish grin lit up her freckled face. "Up for a trip?"

I narrowed my eyes at her. "This wouldn't be like the last time, would it?"

Taylor blew her overly long blond bangs out of her eyes and pouted. "Noooo," her elongated vowel ended with her lips in an exasperated 'O' shape. She threw up her hands as if to emphasize her point. "And you know that wasn't my fault. The computer said the signal was jammed. How was I supposed to know it was a false alarm?"

"Did you double and triple check your readings?" I knew she had. The woman was an absolute savant when it came to anything programmable. Sure I was an engineer and no slouch, but Taylor Wayne lived, breathed, ate, and slept tech. I, on the other hand, loved the mechanical. Give me a machine, and I'd make it work. Then, Taylor would give it life—well, a cyber one.

"Oh so that's how you want to play today?" Narrowing those hazel eyes at me, she waved at Grace. "Dr. Harper, I think you need to take her to the med bay. Clearly, my friend here is suffering from some type of delusional episode."

The poor doctor looked between us as if unsure what to do.

"Don't worry, Grace. She's kidding." I shook a finger at Taylor. "No scaring our doctor. And besides, you've been known to slack off a time or two." That was a complete lie, but riling up my friend was my favorite hobby. And she was so much easier than any of my sisters.

"You!" She spun away and started down the hall. "I'm not falling for your tricks, Sage. You're either coming or you're not."

I glanced helplessly at Grace for backup. Her toothy smile returned, and she shrugged. "Well, you could always still come with me for that check-up."

My mouth dropped open in horror. Clamping it shut, I stared at her. "No offense, Doc, but I'm off!" Chasing after Taylor, I shot like an arrow released from the bow. "Tay! Wait for me!"

The trip to the satellite station was blessedly short. With my big sister, better known as Captain Jane Kadaran, pulling rank and accompanying our little space flight, the two-seater shuttle was cramped. Since Jane flew and Taylor had called shotgun, I was stuck slumping in the pull down seat behind them.

"Why are you here again?" I said with no attempt to hide my irritation. I loved Jane, truly. But when she barked orders like she owned every corner of the galaxy, I wanted to scream. I didn't begrudge her being in charge. She was an amazing captain and earned her rank through no small trials. However…

"I don't answer to you, Lieutenant." Her midnight blue eyes narrowed as she shot me a look over her shoulder.

That attitude of hers rubbed my patience raw. "Listen, Captain." I sucked my teeth. "Taylor and I have this completely under—"

"Ladies," Taylor interrupted. "As much as I'd love to grab some popcorn for this sibling spat, we have a job to do."

Jane grunted as she steered the ship into the satellite station's docking bay. Killing the engine and opening the hatch, we all shuffled free. I had to push the passenger seat forward on its mechanical wheels to pass through the door.

Taylor's giggle softened her earlier words as she continued where she left off, "Besides I want to hear more about our aliens."

"They're not *our* aliens." I rolled my eyes. Ever since the Rhonar, a race of alien warriors, had made contact a few short weeks ago, all anyone could talk about was them—and their offer.

Jane muttered under her breath but loud enough for me to hear, "They might be."

Latching onto her arm, I forced her to stop in her tracks and look at me. "Say what now?"

"I can't say." She shook me off and continued forward.

"Oh no you don't." I circled around her, arms crossed over my chest. "You're not getting away with that. What do you mean?"

Jane sighed. "Do you know what they're after?"

I huffed. Everyone on the moonbase and Earth knew about the aliens. When the Rhonar first found us, they claimed to have discovered the fate of our lost deep-space flight. We hadn't heard from it in months and feared the worst. As it turned out, we were right to be afraid. The starship had been attacked and the whereabouts of most of the crew were still unknown. Only one survivor had been recovered—saved by a Rhonar warrior. To say we were skeptical was an understatement, but the holo-vid from the human scientist and member of the deep-space flight, Ava May Kouris, reassured us. Dr. Kouris hadn't been back to Earth yet, but she was already a celebrity. Reproductions of her holo-vid were plastered everywhere with the title, *First Contact Achieved*, in bold letters. Although Earth knew about aliens, only the moonbase personnel knew the gritty details of what they wanted.

"Brides," I choked on the word. As a modern, 22nd century woman, I wasn't ready to be a mail-order bride for some alien race—even if Dr. Kouris' classified section of the holo-vid made it all sound like a fairy tale. I wasn't buying into fated mates and cosmic connections. My feet remained firmly planted on the ground, although I lived in space. But whatever, I was a practical engineer, not a fantasy princess. "And we're compatible."

Then again, after the punctures in the atmosphere, the decreased land masses and minimal availability of livable space on Earth, the diminishing overall population and the vast outnumbering of the female populace, our options were dwindling. I couldn't afford to be a prude about this, if it meant humanity's survival.

"Yes," she said stoically as we headed toward the outer rim of the satellite. "Now that our geneticists have deemed it possible to reproduce—"

Taylor clapped her hands together in mock excitement. "How romantic."

Jane pinned her with a stare.

Taylor gulped.

"As I was saying," Jane continued, waving us to walk and talk. "The Rhonar believe we humans may have evolved from one of their lost colonies. Whether or not that's true, we know we're a genetic match with these aliens. And since the human male population is…"

"Slim pickings," I filled in for her helpfully, a smirk curling my lips.

"Yes." She sucked her teeth. "And the Rhonar have the opposite problem—"

"Hold up!" Taylor interjected. "They don't have women?"

Jane sighed. "Are you both going to let me finish, or should I keep this restricted?"

In tandem, Taylor and I made a zipping motion over our mouths. Then, I wiggled my fingers for her to go on.

"Fine. But one more interruption and this conversation is over." She pinned us with that captain's no-nonsense gaze. "Anyway, this is all being declassified as we speak. Our babbler implants have received a global update to be sure we can communicate efficiently. And the GAN plans to broadcast the Rhonar's offer to the women of Earth."

After the catastrophes on our planet, the world's governments eventually got their acts together and joined forces. It resulted in the Global Alliance of Nations with a panel of elected officials that ran the remaining habitable areas, controlling resources and ensuring law and order. It wasn't perfect but after the barbarism I'd read about in history books, it was probably the best governance humanity had since our existence began.

"So, what do we get in exchange for sending women to be breeders?" I couldn't control my cynicism. Mom said it was my most charming trait. She was bias.

"No one is going to be a breeder, Sage." The good captain transformed back to big sister quickly with that exasperated statement. "And no Rhonar are allowed on Earth or the moonbase. If they're staying," she began to tick items off her fingers, "they have to make their own habitable station, provide us with schematics of their advanced technology, and introduce us to potential alien trading partners."

"Why do we need all that?" Taylor's hazel eyes widened so much they made her appear like a blond owl.

"We're getting in the weeds here, ladies." Jane ran a hand through her hair. It was the exact shade of an acorn and never failed to poof, despite her attempts to tame it.

I secretly envied her hair, although I'd never admit it to her. Mine was a boring flat brown in comparison. Each of my sisters was a beauty in her own right, which made me feel like the ugly duckling sometimes. I mean I loved my full figure. I rocked my curves, and I worked hard at my confidence, but did all my sisters have to be beauty queens?

My mother, a single woman who had desperately wanted kids, adopted the four of us over the course of a year when we were all little. Even though we weren't biologically related, we were as tight as any sisters could be, which meant arguments, jealousy, and competition. But a lot of love too. I'd kill or die for my sisters, no question. And Taylor was an honorary sibling.

But right now… "Jane please stop pulling the captain card." I pointed to the area outside the satellite where I spotted the problem. "There's a clog in the com dish, some space debris, and I'd like to get it fixed and back to the moonbase before I turn thirty."

"Fourty-two days!" Taylor cheered a bit too happily.

"Are you counting down?" I asked, incredulous.

She pinched my cheek. "Of course, my little wizened one. Then you can be an old lady with me."

At four months my senior, Taylor wasn't old, but she loved to tease me. Now, Jane on the other hand…

"Pssh." Jane snapped. "If you two are old, what does that make me?"

Taylor stared at me helplessly.

I shook my head. "Oh no, you stepped right into that. I'm not touching it with a ten-foot poll." At only eighteen months older, Jane and I weren't far apart in age. But she had always taken on the elder sister job with relish. As a natural leader, it fit her.

"Forget it, Specialist." Shaking off the comment, Jane opened the cabinet for the space gear. "Let's get to work."

Leaning toward me, Taylor half-whispered, half-cried. "She used my title!"

"You're fine." I laughed, knowing Jane was just shifting into work mode.

Taylor made a mewling noise but stayed silent thereafter.

I hung back and stared through the satellite station's wide curved windows. The clog in the communications dish didn't look too bad. Once I got out there, I was sure I could fix it fast. A shadow danced in the distance, close enough to make out a triangular outline, but far enough not to see the details.

"Aliens," I said softly. It was still tough to imagine. But there they were, flying just beyond reach. I wondered, not for the first time, what they were like. So far they'd been in negotiations with our top officials, but to my knowledge, no one had actually seen them beyond fuzzy holo-vids. At least, if they had, no one was talking. Our technology wasn't as advanced as theirs. "Guess their DNA is right though." I couldn't believe our government agreed to test reproductive compatibility. But our scientists exchanged samples and both species agreed. We could make babies.

I scoffed. That was the last thing on my mind. I mean I liked kids, but I had plenty of time. No biological clock ticking for me, thank you. I rubbed my forearm absently.

"Here you go, Lieutenant." Jane's voice broke me from my thoughts, and I turned from the window. She had readied my jumpsuit while Taylor procured my toolbox.

I smiled, taking the items from them. "Thanks. This is always my favorite part of the job."

"You do seem in your element out there." Taylor shivered at the space beyond the window. She might work on the moonbase, but the vastness of space was not her jam.

I, on the other hand, loved every ounce of it. The wide open and endless sea of space with its speckle of stars ignited my dreams. I might be pragmatic, but I had an active imagination. "I am."

"Then, get it done, sis." Jane gave me a one-armed hug. "And be safe."

I hugged her back and grabbed Taylor with my free arm. A slither of awareness crept along my spine. I squeezed them tighter and glanced over Jane's shoulder. Outside the window another shape sped through the darkness. It didn't appear like the steady triangular ship that patrolled the skies. It had a different feel to it, more…unsettling. It flew deeper in space as if hiding in the depths. If I had not been staring in that direction, I would have missed it. A small part of me wondered if I imagined it.

Not wanting to jinx my mission or worry my sister and friend, I pulled back and put as much confidence into my words as I could. "Let's go for a space walk."

Don't stop now. Keep reading with your copy of ALIEN'S MATE.

And if you'd like to connect about the Earth Brides & Alien Warriors series with other readers, I'd love to have you join my Reader Group.

Want even more behind-the-scenes access with exclusive content, spicy art, steamy scenes, special discounts, and more? Check out my Patreon for all the details.

between the alien warriors and Earth break before it's even begun? And if it does, how will I ever be with this alien who's slowly stealing my heart?

Only the stars know.

Acknowledgments

To say this book was a labor of love is not enough. It takes a village, and mine came in the form of two years of kindness and support from the sci-fi romance community before I ever put my fingers to the keys. Thank you to every author and reader whose excitement for a book that wasn't even written led me to finally make the leap into this genre. You are an incredible group of people.

Special shoutout to Alison Aimes for being the actual sweetest person on the planet. If you haven't read her books, do it now, seriously. And to Ava Ross, who spent two hours on a Friday morning chatting with me about all things alien. Everything she writes is gold. Much love to all of these incredible authors who you must read: Tana Stone, Ella Maven, Annabelle Rex, Honey Phillips, V. K. Ludwig, Tasha Black, SJ Sanders, and the amazing group of authors I will undoubtedly and unintentionally leave off this list, you can see my Goodreads SFR for all of them.

To Danielle DeVor and Yelena Casale who, despite my ridiculous, last minute plea of pure insanity, agreed to beta read this book for me. You two wonderful humans would make any alien happy, but I'm so glad you're here on Earth because I would be utterly lost without you.

To my hubs, thank you for letting me work with only the occasional grumblings, and for making my health a priority. If not for you, I'd be slumped over a keyboard every night, and despite my desire to be an actual cybernetic author, I appreciate your watchful eye. I love you to the stars and back, even if you're not an alien.

To my fab five, what would I do without our weekly gabfests? Whether it's marketing tips, writing advice, or plain old fun, I look forward so much to our talks. So, Danielle Bannister, Hannah Bryon, Sherri Hayes, and Marianne Morea, thank you for getting me through an absolutely chaotic year. May your dreams always be as unending as the universe, but close enough so you reach them all.

To my team, you all are the reason why I do what I do, why I get out of bed in the morning, why I speak passionately to anyone who will listen about books. Authors, editors, partners, and friends, you inspire me more than you'll ever know, and I appreciate you more than I can ever show you. If ever you doubt yourself, remember I believe in you, and you are a shining star.

To my family and friends, thank you in advance for **never** reading this book. While I am more than proud to take on the title of "Purveyor of Alien Smut," and I appreciate your support, I do not need to explain to grandma about alien pickles, or to your children about why their aunt loves naked man-chest covers. Love you, now put the book down.

To my readers, now you can read **all** the books! And I love you for it. Your emails, social media comments, and reviews give me so much energy, and I cannot thank you enough for them. Without readers, I'm typing these words into the void. And no Rhonar wants to be in the void. Thank you for loving sci-fi romance and traveling with me amongst the stars. Until the stars align, and we meet again!

About the Author

TINA MOSS s a USA Today Bestselling Author of urban fantasy, paranormal romance, and sci-fi romance. She lives in NYC with a supportive husband and corgi Bear, though both the males hog the bed and refuse to share the covers. Her corgi Chuck now lives in her heart. When not writing, she enjoys reading,  watching cheesy horror flicks, and traveling. As a 5'1″ Shotokan black belt, she firmly believes that fierce things come in small packages.

www.tinamoss.com

www.ingramcontent.com/pod-product-compliance
Lightning Source LLC
Chambersburg PA
CBHW031336010826
48972CB00012B/696